A Letter From Latıka
&
Locker No.11

{Yes..., Latika a prostitute.....not.... by choice}

By

TAPAN MAJHI

Also by
TAPAN MAJHI

1st: Sambhabanara Sakala (Odia Poem)

2nd: Ohh! (Odia Storybook)

3rd: Ohh! (English Story)

4th: Astalagna (Odia Poem)

*5th: Imperfect Love Story Always Untold
(English Novel)*

6th: My Workaholic Wife (English Novel)

About the Author

Tapan Majhi. (B.Sc., MBA)

One who can paint on the canvas of reality and one of the mornings of many possibilities is the writer Tapan Majhi. He asks for a handful of rolling ages, writes something for the betterment of the environment, and continually seeks to recreate this creative treasure. Tapan's voice, style, and presence are apparent in the company of contemporary youth.

On the other hand, he works on a modern ODIA poem where a new poetic idiom expresses an overwhelming sense of malaise, despair, and cynicism that will set a new trend for contemporary literature. Time and again, the subtle realization of life has become the cornerstone of his story. The writer, the eldest son of Dayanidhi Majhi and Kuntala Majhi, is a resident of Avana village in Baleshwar District of Odisha, India, and is currently working in the banking sector.

Know more about TAPAN MAJHI by visiting:

https://facebook.com/tapanmajhi.kumar
amazon.com/author/tapanmajhi
Mail: tapansahitya@gmail.com
tapanmajhi.com
Threads/Instagram : tapanmajhivlog

Dedicated to:

That girl who spoiled her life.

Once upon a time, she told me.

"I am a prostitute not by choice......but....by chance."

Contents

Prologue

Once upon a time, I saw on a signboard that *female species are more dangerous than males,* which was written with a modern nude girl photo. Is it true in such a male-dominated society? If it's true, then why does every column of breaking news contain dried pictures and death messages for females? It may be true or false, but my esteemed readers will decide the aftermath. In my view and experience, I have never noted my dairy. She was a simple, carefree girl playing with her friends, and time and tides never allowed her to realize her childhood. She was bound by family responsibility. She was never cared for by any of her caring relatives. All came and dragged benefits with opportunities. She is the girl Latika. She faced many hurdles and obstacles but was defeated or died, which God knows. Yes..., she was a prostitute by chance, not by choice. How long will she sustain torture and humiliation? Her true lover does not recognize her first love. Both of their family members ignored her soft revolutions. Respecting society, she got married to a negligent fellow. Such a lax character and heedless person never tries to see her inner heart of love. She was tortured by her first husband and inlaws' relatives. She was bound to leave her first husband with dairy blame. She wants to live a caring, individual life. But not saved by the solidarity of society's eyes. She was again burdened with obeying for a second marriage and left home with new hope. The second marriage with the second husband did not respect her thoughts and beliefs. Torture leads to such an extent that she finds herself in a red-light area.

There, she met Patralekha, who sheltered her for safety and secured the life she gained in an NGO, a shelter house. The pseudo-eyes of the charitable organization proved their integrity. There, she garnered with annoyance, which compelled her to come back to the redlight area. Their better and bitter experiences forced them to restore their destination, and pilgrims came to satisfy their unavoidable needs for inexplicable reasons in exchange for money. Still, she was searching for true love and belief. Again, she trusts another guy, Rounak. He cheats on her cunningly and escapes.

She thought her life was already spoiled. Let's try to rewrite the life of Patralekha again. She took her to native. Family members and others never respect their expectations. Patralekha went to the house of her dance teacher. She saw the pathetic life of that person who made her life so drastic. Patralekha left her home permanently. They spent their own life with as they wished. But luck and life never gave her more time. All hopes dried and scorched. Patralekha suffered and died of cancer. Latika became alone. Getting much humiliation, hate, detest, and torment vituperate her mind and soul. So, she has made a bold decision that may depart from the materialistic world. She wrote a letter to her beloved in which she bags to state her true love and belief. Mute revolution against her opponent, which justifies how true love vanished without nurture and nourishment of dual support.

Yes, clap never sounds without two faces of hand. A lover would never be a gladiator without the support of a companion. Why was Latika walking alone? Why was mental and moral support devastated by her near and dear? Patralekha shows solidarity by supporting her to any extent. Why Patralekha! What for Patralekha! When Patralekha....Sorry, a prostitute came into the picture to change the whole story and clean garbage from society.

Let's enjoy the novel by cementing each one mind with Latika and the consequence of the letter giving the proper judgment to

"A Lettre From Latika & Locker No. 11"

Part 1

Hi...Dear...Darling,

How are you...?

I am not here to repeat anything. Next time you will not get a chance to tell me..... I am **on cloud nine**. It's not my **crocodile tears**. I will no longer be in this Hippocrates atmosphere. Suffocation is better than a permanent vacation. Why did I decide to die? Not for you, not for my husband, and also not for my relatives. I am not here to blame my society, where people burn statues while alive and worship after death. Life and achieving a goal are not on the same path or not in my palm. There is no shortcut to success. Or change life as we wish. You can't catch **a crow fly**.

Yes, it was a lovely day ...when I was a baby. My cry is heaven's anguish, and a smile is heaven's joy. All well loved me. I felt God had created me, such a unique prince. My first cry did not astonish my family members but upset neighbors' minds. My parents were thrilled. Yes, it was a trend or tradition ... I don't know. The public has a negative impression of the birth of a girl's child as I am ***the black sheep of my Family***. Still, some praise and assuring the birth of a child is a symbol of wealth and prosperity. Goddess Maa Laxmi comes to our family. But my parents could not read their Pseudo thoughts. Gradually, that conversation made them happy. My father never smiles. ***Once in a blue moon,*** he smiles. I was the root cause of his smiles. I don't know ...why she loved me very much.

Generally, father loved girls very much. I could not be out of nature. My childhood was running with simple living without high thinking. I just started walking with my little feet and slowly running with the guidance of my parents and others. I was highly cared for not only by my family members but also by my surroundings.

Sometimes, my elders and grandpa (Grandfather) tell me –I am the property of others. One King will come and take me to his palace with his chariot. I will be the queen of his dynasty. Alas! You are not that fortunate. Someone caught me, and his restrictions bound my time, which compelled me to make this hard decision. I don't know. In the future, will you meet me or not? Let's leave it...I never expected you would come to me, and I would be yours and mine. But you did not allow me to prove my love and never yourself as you are for me. Why does a girl fall in love? If love has such an ending as mine, Pritam ..., I don't know what you think about me, but I forever have a wrong impression of you. I can't forget you because you are

***cheek by jowl*-**day by day.

Yes... Pritam, I remember that day. It was 5 p.m., and I played with other children in my colony. I was immersed in dust and mud. You came with your mother. Your mother's house is in our colony. Rarely did you come. It was not on my notice. With your presence, my mother snatched me from that playground and beat me very carefully. I cried and cried. But you were laughing at me. Your Mother protects me with love and care. I had a little fight with my mother. My mother scolds me and beats me again for my notorious activities. Your silent look told me *–**Why cut off your nose to spite your face?***

After some time, your mother washed and cleaned my body. I bathed again. I never forgot your mother as she cared for me a lot. I am obliged and thankful to her. If she were alive now, you would not be a cheater. It was my bad luck or your good luck....That God knows.

Tell me, Pritam...you made this mistake. Yes, it was not your mistake...you made a blunder that will never be erased. You have never given me any option. I also tried to ***turn over a new leaf***.

But time and tide wait for none, and how does it respect my thoughts and feelings? You are always searching for a safe zone for yourself. You are very self-conscious, like other guys. No one took offense, so you are always ***tongue-in-cheek***. Whatever it may be. I wish you a happy, prosperous life. Today is my last day. I am going to die or to be hanged till death. The court gives the order to fulfill his last wish. I am unfortunate to get this opportunity. Because I am not here to die by a court order but my wish to spoil life. Yes... I am the scapegoat of this family. Everyone's problem will not be solved if I do not die. But I had one wish to meet you before leaving this world. So I will write all these things and will you get this letter or not...that's God knows.

Yes, I forgot about that evening when my mother scolded me and your mother cared for me. Their separate respect evolved from the bottom of my heart towards my mother. Your mother called my mother as sister. My father is the brother of your mother, in a distant relationship. Your mother comes to our house *once in a blue moon.*

So I have met your mother very few times. But the first time I met you. I was irritated by looking at your satire and laughing. But your mum softly scolded my mother.

Why are you beating? So cute..... Baby.

: Sister. You don't know. She is getting arrogant and audacious in all activities.

: A child is like that. Beating or threatening is not the solution. They need care and love every moment.

: I can't. Care, such a naughty baby. You take care.

: Ok...Don't...Worry...After twenty years. I will take her to my home as my daughter-in-law. At that time, you were caring for my daughter-in-law. My son will marry your daughter.

After listening to your mother's nice and caring statement, I cried. I told her I would not leave my mum. I will not marry. I will go nowhere.

Your mother assured me –No, I will not take you to my home. You stay here.

I stayed at home. You and your mother went to your uncle's house. On that day, I heard about marriage. This divine function divides one relationship and builds a new one.

That morning, I played with all my childhood friends. You also joined the company. We played with sand, mud, and a small utensil.

We call everyone not by name but by relationship. We had a separate family. On that day, a local festival was observed. That was Kumar Purnima (Full moon day). This autumn festival is the most famous and popular in our village. The God of War lord Murugan was born on that day. This day is celebrated among girls. A traditional ritual is when girls pray for their best life partner. I remembered ...we were playing beneath the light of the moon.

You also joined us. We dance with old folklore *"Kuanra ... Punei Janha lo... Phula Baula Beni...."*

I was your bride on that day, and you were my groom.

Everything was running like a child's game. After the game is over, life is over. The next day, it started as it was. Gradually, you became very **cheek-by-jowl**. You became my best friend. Separate confidence and self-respect have developed from the inertia of my mind. I was a teen girl. You are at the age of eighteen. You are already my closest friend, not a friend, but more than that.

Teenage people bear some specialties in everyone's life. How will I get out of that? I got my first menstruation cycle. I was afraid of getting into such a bloodbath. I cried and told my mother about such an incident. My mother gave me a confused laugh, and I was confused. I was separated from others—a line of restriction drawn around me. Without bathing, I would not touch anything or anyone. My mother gave me new clothes and told me to go to the bathroom. I bathed fully in cold water as it was an evening in autumn. I felt a little cold. When I came out of the bathroom after some time, I was the center of attraction for my elders. Their squirrel smiles put me in a dilemma. I can't understand. What was happening to me? I didn't dare to ask my mother. I shied with fear. Priest did a small puja (Worship) that evening at my home. On that day, a Brahmin came to our home.

I was sitting near that podium. Some elders bless me by putting their hands on my head. Two of my three teenage sisters laughed at me. I was in a dilemma. Why is a girl bloodbath like me? It was the first day of my life with the red carpet treatment. After dinner, my mother told me to stay home and not go outside. I did not go to the puja room, temple, or other holy places. I feel cursed. The first time I used a sanitary napkin. It discomforted me. I used to change up to seven days.

Oh..! Sat... Why am I writing shy secrets to you? Every girl feels too shy when saying these things. Still, I am telling you... Why? I don't know ... Pritam. What are you thinking about me? This is the immersive fact of a lady always unsaid. Still, I am telling you not to enjoy it. To clarify from day one how I loved you. Later, I know my body is ready to accept the reproductive system. I can deliver a baby. I may be the mother of your child. But medical science does not permit my biological system also. *I was still **in the pink** of health.* My body is not allowed, but my mind always needs you.

I can't understand where the mistake is.

Why did you do it?

You terminated the history between you and me and sacrificed the present. I did not create a shadow of doubt in the blue sky of your faith by looking at your charming face, dashing style, and gorgeous body. So why do I remember you today?

Love – Bonding, inner feelings, and Endearment Excitement were all literary festivals. So why weren't the family members in my favor? You would have been a symbol of struggle.

I know that a woman who symbolizes revolution or struggle takes the form of Sati Sita or Yagyanseni. However, the dream of building a family cannot be realized. So you say...? Was it my mistake to be harsh towards you?

Not wrong..... Everyone in this world thinks me wrong. By mistake, if I ever talk about your love and turn over the pages of the history of my love with someone who walks with me...with great hope and reliance.

But, neither can I understand nor can you make me recognize that their (your and my family member's) brutal murder of my love is the reason for the close bond between us.

So, I will say that I am neither guilty nor innocent. I silently witnessed the story of famous writer Bibhuti Patnaik's (Premika)' Girlfriend.' Anyway, your last letter killing my memories of the lovebird sitting in the garden of my heart's city has tormented me like (Pitamaha Bhisma) a dejected gladiator by the questionnaire of doubt, hate, and deception. I am not 'Lord Siva'. I will create new mythology by drinking your hate and detest.

You believe me ... Pritam...I am never **green *with envy*.**

Yes, I don't like to discuss these nonsense things, but why am I constantly repeating and making mistakes regularly?

You may say it's my soft corner to get you. I strongly agree it's my deepest love forever. You love or detest... The winning part is always on my side.

"If you love me, I will be in your heart........

If you hate me, I will be in your mind."

Many things happened. Still, I am waiting for you with my celestial eye. Everyone in society has the character of Draupadi. Why do I have a characterless certificate from others? Are you solely responsible for my divine love or selfish sex?

Nowadays, sex is a common thing for me. You don't know how often I spent my body on a single penny. Now, I am a well-known prostitute. Who is selling my body every day and night? It's tough to digest by listening to this word. Each of my muscles...sorry, not muscle ...the rotten flesh was sold on the market in premium currency. The cells of my body were more than spiritual thoughts of my body. Because no one had come here to study my mind...all is with a hope of sexual satisfaction and an inner nasty desire.

So, you tell me how I can serve with noble thoughts. Every night, I was served dinner by a different customer. As you know, I belonged to an impoverished rural family. How do I know different sexual poses to satisfy a burning desire? Sometimes, I was bitten by a notorious consumer.

Still, I like your celestial love and care. I never found any paid customers.

I remember one night, my health was not good. I was feeling hungry. My burning stomach needs some food. No one gave a piece of bread. Instead of getting food, I had to pay for myself. Finally, I got a diet.

You have no idea about me. This is a different industry. You may say,... society of slums. But every night, all sex mongers come here with new hope and desire. Underneath the blue light, everyone is immersed in a burning passion, which you can't say love. It's purely sex. I liked it every day.

A night with colorful arrangements invites many industrialists, politicians, doctors, engineers, the business community, young professionals, students, and tourists. Every buyer purchases the best out of the worst. Here they all were with a jolly mind and left before the sun rose in the morning. Why does all sex hunger love darkness? It is sex coming from the dark, or it creates sex stimuli in the inertia of the mind. Whatever it may be, all are left with a happy and free mind and also giving again return commitment.

Why am I telling you that unseen truth to you? So why will I not tell you? You should know why I chose or forcefully came here to choose.

You must see many stories like mine when you come to this nasty dynasty. No one is here by their own choice. Such a profession is not by choice but by chance.

I do not belong to those unfortunate girls who lost

their virginity before they cared. Chastity has no value to be judged by anybody. Everything is measured by satisfying willpower and erotic expression. Here are many bed partners of the same customer. There are a variety of beds with different charges. The customer paid royal, deluxe, and honeymoon charges, among many other things. Wholenight charges are more costly than other charges.

Wait, Pritam...I will not say many things in a short span of breath. You can't understand or digest it. After listening to this, your mind must have a negative vibration. Obviously...., It's not new to you. Every holy, simple mind is like that. After reading my letter, don't panic. I am not yours. If you love me ...it's the bow of our first love. Never be in the hate dairy. I was forced to do it....sorry... it's not like that. I came with my unknown friend. She kept me as her sister as she has been here for the last thirty-two years. She had not been in the same profession since her childhood. She was from a remote area of the northeast. She got married at the age of eight. A man from Mumbai came to the northeast region for the tea business. Motivate their parents and get married. You may say it's a child marriage. It's a crime.

How is that possible? Everything is possible in our country. Child labor on pen and paper was abolished, as per government records. Go through the metro market, tea garden, small factory, etc., and you will know everything. Starvation and poverty compelled us to do this. Their family thought they would get some money if they accepted a marriage offer for their child. Poverty can be eradicated in a few days, and they will have a good son-in-law. Still, their family members are waiting for my friend to return to his house. Now she is in such a stage... not to move forward or backward. It's such a one-way entry where there is no exit. No one has the option or interest in correcting the mistake.

You want to know who my best friend is: sister, mother, guide, philosopher, everything. Sorry, I will not tell you anything. You will find out about her later. I don't want to lose all your interest or desire quickly. I know passion never creates pressure. It will give joy and happiness.

From that happiness, I remember my childhood. I attended my first menstruation cycle. It was great happiness for my family. But my inner desire for fear increases with the increase in the darkness of night. As night increases, my thought process runs with high pulses. Everything got confused. No one was there to answer my questions. Later on, I cleared as the calendar date increased. I am sixteen. Cycling was not new to me. I was conscious and concerned about what to do and what not to do.

As you asked me many times to meet you, I'm cunningly avoiding drawing your attention in different ways.   Yes...this is an example of concern and consciousness. Rules still break my rules and regulations. Many times, you kissed me without my permission. It's not required for a lover to take permission from a loved one. I know my showing of avoiding attitude was caught by your cunning eye because I am not so intelligent enough to study your mind and flying thought process.

Whatever it may be, our childhood was very romantic. So now I am burning with my present youth. No one is here to accompany my societal burden. Now I am walking alone, sitting alone, thinking...singing...everything. Yes, I have to die. Otherwise, I would not justify my birth.

Yes ..Pritam, everything is confusing you. You might have thought what I am telling you. Am I mad....? Yes...I am.

The situation has changed. No one is with me. I am alone, running, walking, and sitting like a madman. Oh.. I am like the solitude of Alexander, who is enjoying or suffering from the word suffer. I remember... In Hindi, suffering means to go long, and suffering in English means getting pain. Both the two words..... You choose the first one and leave the village. I have not decided, but I am bound to accept the other one's suffering. I have pain every day. From today, you will not get any pain. I am taking the whole pain for you, bastard.

Oh...! Sorry... I apologize for my words. I never scold or use this type of language. Yes..., you are not mine, but I am for you ever.

Whether you believe it or not...my beloved Pritam.

Just come and see how my husband damages my private part. Every night, he comes to me only for sexual satisfaction. I am just a playing stone for him. He never realized what a wife is! According to him, a wife will be an incredible instrument forever. It's my fortune that he has not considered an instrument for everyone. If I opened my whole body, you would be astonished by how many cut marks and black spots from cigarettes read on my body. Once upon a time, you kissed there and loved it very much.

Ohh!... I never want to remember these days. I am in tremendous pain. It was my love for you. I was eighteen. You came to meet me **once in a blue moon.** *That* was a full day. It was hot. I couldn't stay at home. I went to my farmhouse with my friend Reena. You came like a thief. Slowly and silently, I entered my house. You touched my chest. I threw out your hand and warned you not to behave inhumanely because Reena slept near me. You dragged me out of the room. We went to the back side of our room. A black rock podium was there. I sat on that. You come and sit near me. I was trembling with fear. My body sweetened out. You came close to me and gave a squirrel sweet kiss on my cheek. Sultrycheeked sweets are delightful. You told me

Wow..., so sweet you are!

I am not a hotcake as you are making these types of comments.

: Still, you are joking and commenting in different ways. I wanted you

: shh!!... Reena is sleeping inside the room. She will come out and broadcast all our secrets to everyone. Just wait a while.

:Hi...don't worry...I locked the room from the outside. She will not come. One day, she will find out our secrets.

You are very conscious of my chastity or your dignity. I asked.

What do you feel like you think? U asked.

After a short discussion, I was very close to you. Moonlight makes my body full of silvery. You tightly embraced my west. Twinkle little stars thought as.....

"Underneath the moonlit sky..., two lovers with one soul already intertwined. Both our hearts were ablaze with passion's fire. We plunged into the journey of love's sweetest romance with tender whispers and stolen glances."

I was getting nervous. I have no interest in opposing you. Both were deducting interest from each other. As our body and mind merged, a version of a symphony of desire ignited with celestial fire. The sweet water bubble from my forehead polished with a cheek of yours. I was slowly lying down, and you were on my breast. We both closed our eyes. I was combing your hair. His long breath got hot and gave me an erotic disorder. You were closely immersed beneath the long hair. It was my first feeling of love. Slowly, slowly, you came to my face. I eagerly cut your lip. It's our honeymoon night...became a sonnet of bliss and a testament to the depth of my eternal kiss.

U asked..!..What are you doing, Latika?

Me: Don't shout...Pritam...This night will never come in the future.

: If you wish... I will come every night.

Every day, I will not come to this farmhouse. My parents went to my relative's house. So, I am here to take care of our crop field. Tomorrow my parents will come back, so you will never get me.

Pritam laughed and laughed.

I asked what happened to your happiness. It was not a simple laugh—just satire.

So...y... you...., protect your crop field from thieves, domestic animals, and wild creatures. But I am one of them who is stealing your property. Who will take care? I am spoiling your holy land.

Why do you think you are spoiling my property? It's a love where there is no ambiguity.

After all, why am I telling you my repeated self-reminders? You never realize that sharing emotion and sentiment makes one's mind free. First, love can't be forgotten. We spent many sweet moments in that farmhouse. It was full of nature and dark beauty. Here, the situation is not like that. Here, the night was full of color and was arranged fully. Still, that time was fantastic. We are both new to a honeymoon night. You can imagine you came to my study room without notice that night. The room was switched off intentionally. A warm welcome is always a new experience. You are very naughty every time. You also tried to open my inner garments. I never opposed it.

**   **

Now, I am an experienced and professional prostitute. Before opening my dress, I dressed down with a sexually appealing pose. My main intention is to bring satisfaction to my customers.

Once upon a time, I was best among others. Now, such charm is not continued. Yes, I am a black rose with a rotten flavor. As age increases, so demand decreases. Who cares about our bodies? It sold like glamour with beauty and sometimes nothing.

When you visit me, you will see how I spend life here. A small room with one bed attached to a washroom, a folded kitchen room with some utensils. One day, it was raining. The town was entirely of water. All vehicles stopped. No customers came to our Redlight colony. I was with no single penny. On that day, I used my body for fifty rupees. That client used me as sugarcane juice ground by a machine. I had no option but to choose anyone. I spent it on myself at a low cost. That was the most challenging situation of my life for bread and butter. During the heavy rain, who came out for entertainment? Everywhere, there was a lockdown.

Which part of my life do you want to hear about? My present without you and my past with you. In both cases, you are not with me. With my past or with my situation. My present situation will not drag you to stand with me. On the other hand, it's not a motivating story that you read for correction.

I was immersed in your love. So, I did not concentrate on my studies properly. When I lived through my literature books, you became a poet for me. When I went through geography...You became a universe for me to study. When I feel free with my history book, I become a gladiator and conquer with others to accomplish my goal.

In all, I lost my concentration and studies. I failed in my exam. I won't blame you for my failure. Because one palm never claps. So blame, I can't share. If you need ...you can participate.

Why did I make a mistake? Only because my parents married an unknown person. Ancient Indian mythology says, "Life is segregated into four parts. The first twenty-five years are **Brahmacharya**. That means a person gathers knowledge and wisdom through education and experience. The second span of life is **Gruhasthya**. That means he completed his schooling and entered into family life. He cares for his spouse, children, and others when he marries. Then the third stage of life is **Banaprastha**. In that stage, a person reduces all his duties and responsibilities. Efficiency and eligibility reduce productivity, which has never garnered as much. Attachment towards belongings faded day by day. The fourth and last stage of life is **Sanyas**. In that stage, a person becomes old. He has no attachment to anyone. I only pray to God for NIRVAN. Many things are written in Indian spiritual science. It was a beautiful life routine designed by our ancestors. Why did I forget duty and responsibility? Of the first stage of my life? Only for that reason has my life twisted in a different direction.

Part 2

It was a sunny morning. I get up from bed with a tired body. I stretched again and went for morning routine work with Reena. But I was not feeling like before. I feel your absence. After bathing, I came home.

I was astonished when I reached home; some unexpected guests sat in our drawing room. One young boy looked very thin and old. They both gave a cold smile. I did not understand. Suddenly, my mother came to me and took me into the room with care. I asked –what happened?

My mom told me – Nothing …you go and dress up with a new sharee.

My confusion enhances the pulse rate of my heart. My cheek and forehead are sweetened with salty water. I was in doubt. Whether my parents married me to that fellow, yes, that was true. Without my interest, they forcefully took me to our dining room. They are both unknown people sitting in front of me. I was bound to bow down my head, and everyone was silent. First time I wore a sharee. I was in doubt whether my private part was looking at anyone or not.

I tightly hold my shares. Suddenly, a question came like a missile.

Are you comfortable cooking food? What is my taste? I am a vegetarian or nonvegetarian.

I was getting silent. I was speechless. One of my aunties was sitting next to me. I became relaxed. No one asked me such a question. By the way, I replied with yes. Finally, that older adult told me to go there. So, I slowly and silently moved out of that place.

But I was listening to what they were talking about me. So, I confirmed that my marriage proposal had come. Why are my parents worried about my marriage? Many discussions happened. From that discussion, I know about that boy who came here to marry me.

He is thirty kilometers from my native country. For the last seven years, he has been working in Gujarat. A lot of cotton industries are there in the state of Gujarat. Almost all people from the northeast states prefer Gujarat for their family's bread and butter. I have no interest in that boy. But the choice was not mine. I made a blunder by not getting a pass on the matriculation exam. If I pass my exam, I must go for higher studies, and these things did not happen to me. Some incidents turn the lives and careers of individuals. I realize education has excellent value.

After some hours, they left and went away. I shouted in the presence of everyone.

I will not marry…it's not my age to go into family life. I oppose this proposal.

An older woman, my mother-in-law, told me she got married at twelve years old. So what's the problem with me? My energy level increases like a mercury thermometer. I oppose many views. Still, everything dissolved like a water bobble. No one listened to my single word. They were all saying –what will we do? You failed a simple exam and have not secured a minimum mark. Who will take care of a young girl simply staying at home? If you get married, then our responsibility will be over.

By listening to the word responsibility, I realized a girl is not an asset to a family. She is always a burden. So I was speechless. That evening, I discussed it again with my parents. To date, I have never talked to my father. Lastly, I politely appeal to my parents. Dear Papa… I am not mentally prepared for marriage.

Father said, "Listen, my baby… I know…you are not mentally prepared. But a good proposal we got. They come to our home with their interest. If we give up, we will not get a good proposal for the future. One better thing is that they have no demand for marriage. I will think of another way if you have passed the exam. An option is not there for us."

It's not in my hands, papa. I will try my best for the next exam. I will do better. –I said.

I can't do anything, so I will not reject the proposal.

He told me to go away and went to dinner.

That night, I did not sleep. Reena was slipping towards me. She tried to convince me a lot. I was thinking about what was happening to me. Why is life going so drastically? Can I retake my life? Who will guide me, and who will take care of my silly, childish nature? Why can't they understand I am immature enough to manage a family? My reproductive organ is not mature enough to deliver a baby after a year.

Whatever it may be, I tried a lot to postpone my marriage... I told my mother that I would not marry any other candidate. Because I loved you very much. After listening to this, my mum slapped me, not once ...more than twice.

My mother, Latika... You are forgetting your family standards and overcoming your line of control. Pritam's mother is my childhood friend. What will she think when she hears all these nonsense things?

I love him very much.... I also replied. Suddenly, my mum growled you can go to any extent... I will not permit you to be this nuisance because I will not draw a black line in my long-term relationship. On the other hand, you should think about your family's caste, background, and status. What will her mother think if I say these things? What do they feel? I am a selfish lady who is using you to take advantage of you.

This is not a benefit ... Mum. I am talking about how your friendship turned into a relationship. Because it's not our one-sided love, we like each other. You again speak to her mother for me before making the wrong decision.

I will not walk with you...you will try your best. I am sure you will get the same reply from her mother. For you, I will not tell her anything. I will not degrade my self-respect and her dignity.

My mother told me her opinion and left the place. Again, I told her in a very polite way, and it made me panic. I decided to go to your house. At least your mum will listen.

The following day, I started my journey to your home. On the way, I practiced what to tell my mother and how to convince her. After a two-hour trip, I reached your home. Reena was with me.

By looking at us, your mum's red carpet was a red letter day forever. She cared for me. I spent more than four hours at your house. Your mum prepared many starters and food for me. I dare to tell your mum about our matter by searching for a suitable time. She asked me what happened... Latika. You are getting nervous.

IAunty... I have a lot of questions on my mind. Will you clarify?

You're Mumyes tell me what you want. Many

confused, doubts and puzzled ideas come to mind these days. After marriage, you will be acquainted with all the problems. Yes, marriage is the panacea of all your remedies. Why do you bother about it?

I am your daughter. What would you do in that situation?

Your Mum —what happened to you ...why...are you asking all these things? Aren't you happy with this marriage?

I genuinely say this is not the expected answer to my question. Please tell me.

She laughed gently. Again tell.

Your Mum — **If** an offer is given to me ... I will take your opinion. Because I have also provided all the liberty to my children, can you tell me which way I can help you?

I –I love your son very much. I want your son forever. Please accept my sincere request.

At that time, your mum was cutting fruit and giving it to me. Looked at me with a very confused eye.

Your Mum —what happened to all these things? When ...how and where? How dare you say these things. If I am not wrong ...you are crossing your limit.

No, these things did not happen on my side. We both agreed to be life partners forever. As he is not here, I am coming to inform you about our relationship. Please help me.

Your Mum —Sorry I can't help you. You must have informed your parents.

I No...no. I only informed my mum. She strongly refused. Because of that, I came here to draw out your kind information. Please accept my request. It's not from my side. Pritam also agreed with me. We are both committed to each other. As he is not there, I am in a dilemma.

Your Mum —I will not permit it. Vehemently denied your offer...request ...demand...whatever it may be. My son is not like that. He will not adjust with you. You are a simple, failed girl. My son is a highly excellent student. His mentality and way of thinking will not match you. On the other hand, you should think about your family background. And our status.

I – Love is different. Love has no caste, creed, color, religion, or status. You may also be your son. He must agree with my words.

Your Mum—stop these nonsense things. I will not permit anyone to degrade my family's goodwill. What I will tell you. By closing my eyes... Your mother must have said the same thing as I told you.

Yes...she is also rejecting my opinion. I have no other way to accomplish my love. So I have come here to express my views. I think you know better than my mother.

Your Mum—you..know why...because I know her. She is not selfish like you. She knows the ethics of friendship. Our friendship has existed for the last thirty-two years. Because our minds and mentalities match each other. What I think is her view..., and what she thinks is mine. What is true love exists in our friendship? What you boys know about love. This is not love, just time passing in your teenage atmosphere. So better to restore your mind. You are invited for lunch at my home, as all the girls visit their relatives' houses before marriage.

And your wishes should never be treated as a decision. You are my loving child, but I can't accept what you think.

On the other hand, Pritam is not self-sufficient to manage a family. If I accept your offer, I will not put his career in a dilemma. You also don't try to keep in touch with him. Your existence in his life may distract you from your destination.

After listening to all these things, I did not expect anything from your mother. I think I will inform your father. So, nothing happened. I know your father is more dangerous and audacious than everyone in your family. I decided to deform with self-thought. After a nice lunch, I left your house just before entering your bedroom. Went through your dairy. I wrote something about my feelings. You must have gone through it. You must measure my celestial love and divine thought. Many best wishes and blessings were assets of mine from your home. Yes, that asset was given to you by your mum. After all, it was a remarkable and memorable experience for my future.

Before evening, I left your house with Reena. While going on the way, I think of many more dreams by looking at the shady sky, greenery crop field, and retired sunset from my duty and how they were deprived of my sorrow.

Since that day, I have not felt comfortable. I don't know what has happened to me. All were showing sympathy to me. Who was commenting and scolding me on any matter? Now they were loving me again. Because I will marry, I will be the property of others—one side's liability transfers to another's asset. So, my life is like a profit and loss account.

Part 3

It was a shining morning with a melodious atmosphere. All were busy everywhere. My parents' faces became gloomy and dry. Because I am going to get married. Today is my wedding function. I went to the pond with all the female members. They took me and sanitized me with oil and turmeric powder. As per Hindu culture and tradition, a girl should bathe in a pot of celestial water with oily turmeric powder. So, she became a holy divine body.

I went home and went to the Puja room. Brahmin started his devotional mantra and worshiping process. After some time, the first phase of the marriage function finished. I went home. I wore new Sharees with different Ornamentals. It is not that all my ornaments are gold or diamond. Most of the jewelry was imitation and mixed gold. Still, I was looking beautiful. But I felt your absence. Gradually, my house became crowded. They were all coming to meet me and present different shares and gifts. Some of my school friends came to me and congratulated me on my new life. Some were wishing me great success and accomplishment.

I did not know what my success was or what my achievement was. Due to my academic failure and misfortune, I will marry my success or, without my choice, getting a new husband is my achievement. So I was in a lot of confusion. Believe it or not... Latika was the only girl who was suffering from sorrow and sadness. Others were happy with pleasure except me.

After some time, the total atmosphere changed with colorful light. Some slow, sonorous sounds enhance my day's dignity. Yes, it was a bright evening at my marriage function. I was sitting on the podium and greeted by many guests and visitors. Night increases with guests and visitors. It was quarter to ten. I went to eat ... all my relatives and guests were enjoying different aromatic food except me. As per marriage rules, I have to fast the whole night. Suddenly, the bomb blasted with an irritating noise and colorful light. All were astonished. Some lady came to me and took me into the room. They told us the groom's team had just arrived near our house. As a new bride, you should not move here and there. I had to go and get well dressed.

After some time, I entered my room. Some girls came to me. Again, I redressed and remade myself. Suddenly, some fear developed in my body. I felt heavy blood circulation and air respiration and trembled with fear.

Slowly, my room became empty—everyone left by saying different work and assignments. The primary purpose was to see their team's groom and dance program because someone was the center of attraction at my marriage function. I was alone. A small line of tears came out. Then, my eyes thoroughly watered. I closed my eyes. Sitting on the bed. What will I do? I am the first lady who is mourned for suffering from a lot of stress and tension in your absence. The melodic atmosphere makes me impatient. Suddenly, I guess someone entered my home. Slowly, I opened my eyes. I found a well-known and unclear figure with my torn eye. You came. It's a miracle, or I am dreaming of your presence. Suddenly, you came to me. An unknown smile came to my face. Your face became tired with a sorry figure. You told me

U: How are you?

Me: Nothing special. I am a catalyst for everyone's happiness.

U: why not with me?

Me: You are not a part of their happiness.

U: Why did you make such a heartbreaking decision? Are you happy?

Me: You tell me what I can do. I tried my best.

I have no words to say. I was on such a stage to move up or down. I was a unique center of attraction. You can see how I am glazed with different ornaments and my new Shares. All the colorful arrangements are only for me. I am the only root cause of all happiness that I require. This remarkable day comes once in a lifetime with joy. –I said.

Suddenly, you cried.

ME: Why are you crying? Are there any blunders? It's good what is happening and will be good ...what has to happen.

So you are not angry with my voice, and you asked why you didn't inform me?

Me: What extra happened to me? I have already tried my best to reach you. It's my bad luck or your good luck ... whatever it may be ..it will be best with time. I have already forgotten about you.

U: So I have to return to my hostel. Why will I be here?

Me: who told ...you to return? What happened ...It's not my fault or your mistake. We respect time.

Immediately, my mum entered our home. She was looking nervous with fear.

I said – Don't worry..mum. Nothing will happen to us. What do you think should not be like that? I will not do such activities, which will hamper our families. Please trust me. ...you leave me ...I had some discussion with Pritam.

Suddenly, mother left us.

You know very well. After that, you demand many things. But I refused to go with you. You tell me, how could I? My future husband had already reached the front of my gate. The welcome ceremony continued. You told me ... was it possible to leave with you? You came close to me and tried to embarrass me. Suddenly, I pushed you back with care.

U Are you getting mad... Latika. What is happening to you?

Me: You have no right to touch me ... Pritam. I sanitized with Ganga jal(Holy water), a different flavor of natural cosmetic powder—a divine soul inside me. If you touch me, then I have to purify again. Don't think I hate you. But it's not the right time to make another mistake.

U so ... I am leaving this function. I will not meet you anymore.

I object to you going out. You threw my hand again...and.... Again. I object to moving an inch. At last, I won. You sit near a corner table. Your face became distressed. You cried. Some tears came out of your eyes. I am close to you. Wipe your eyes full of tears with my shares. You looked at me and said

What happened? You told me that ... You... Would you not come to me? Even touch me. What is this?

Me: Keep patience... Pritam. My purpose in talking is not what you think. I am going to get married. I pushed you not to convert my love into hate and detest. I was yours...and forever. Every love never ends with marriage. There are some relationships beyond love and emotion. I am not saying we are unfortunate. Our love story is spiritual and eternal, like Radha and Krishna, Krushna and Krishna.

So why did you worry about me? What a bold decision I took. It's not for me. Or am I not selfish? Many lives are disturbed. If I married you, you could be unfit and self-sufficient to manage a family. If we both made a wrong decision by neglecting others, you and I would be unhappy. Think about others. What will be the status and dignity of your family? The relationship between my family and your family will be in jeopardy. People must comment on the friendship between your mother and your Mum. So, better your future and my good luck, I made such a bold decision.

U: So...all the best for your promising future. I am leaving this melodious atmosphere. So, no one can blame me. On the other hand, I am suffocated here by looking at your face.

Me: Yes, I am not supplemental oxygen for you. You may leave. Now, I will oppose it. Because I not only love you but also trust you. For the sake of my love and belief, I accept such a truth. I expect at least you will care for me unquestioningly. Because outside the room, a lot of rumors are being spread. If you do not all attend my marriage function, people and my relatives will think there is something between us. You expect ...! I will always blame you. Why do you tarnish my chastity? I wish you to take me to the marriage podium as my superior, guide, beloved, and well-wisher. You stop everyone's mouth forever. I can't leave without you. I will be your Radha, and you will be my Krishna forever. Our love should be divine, celestial, and eternal. I request that you complete a secret assignment.

After some time, all the girls and relatives suddenly entered the room. They are all hurrying to take me to Mandapam(Podium). I slowly object to others to keep patience. You raise your hand to assist me. I also tied up with your hand. You walked slowly and slowly, and I was behind you. Others were walking behind me. I bent my head. You drop me at marriage Mandapam. My groom was sitting beside me. All became silent. Your presence had already stopped confusion in everyone's minds. After leaving me, you sat near the corner chair. Brahmin chanted mantras with a loud voice.

Yes... marriage is a sacred union between two individual souls. It's not a societal note or contract. I didn't know an ample sense of unity characterizes such a marriage. After some time, my marriage ceremony was over. In between my marriage program, I tried to find you in the crowd. My watery eyes are not able to search for you.

I was sure that you may have left that area. You are

exceptionally sentimental and softhearted. You are unable to digest the situation. From that night to that date, you went and never returned. I didn't try to find you anywhere in my busy, routine life. So this is the last time I am writing to you to tell you many things. After my marriage, I took my relatives to the bride's room. I took food. I was getting tired. Midnight was already covered. The morning sky looks pretty dark. The sun may appear after some time. I will come after some time. It was harrowing for me to adjust to the atmosphere. We all cried. Because I am leaving my home, my parents, friends, and relatives, including my barnyard, this place holds all the memories from birth to till date. It comes into everyone's life, especially for brides. The bride prejudice session had already started. Before leaving, I went to meet my father.

He was standing silent. I cried and cried. A strong and bold man ...my father became a broken bamboo.

All his strength and boldness dissolved into a drop of water. He cried impatiently like a child. I also gave some advice on managing my family without hesitation.

After some time, I went to my mother's house. She was crying like mad. All my relatives were crying, including me. My inlaws' side assured my parents and relatives – nothing would happen. Your daughter will be thrilled and comfortable. We will take care of your child as our daughter. She will not feel any difference between us.

With much assurance and commitment, I departed

from the hearts of my family members. I was forcefully dragged into the chariot. My husband was sitting adjacent to me. All my friends and relatives were crying while looking at me. This was the last valedictory situation from my native. Suddenly, the door closed, and the chariot moved forward. Some melodious sound gets dissolved into sonorous. Everything turned into pin-drop silence. After some time, I closed my eyes and slept. After a long, long, I woke up. Some unknown touches I felt. Suddenly, I opened my eyes. I saw that no one was there. My husband was sitting near to me and kept his hand on my shoulder gently. I also bow my head toward his chest. Why, I felt some care and belongingness. I had already reached near to my mother-in-law's house. The sun rises from the east. Sunshine has matured. I looked at my watch. It was Quarter to Eight.

Part 4

Their family members warmed me. When I entered into their family, I felt something new. Slowly, my sorrow and pain faded with their family members' attachment. Everyone in his family cared for me. I was the center of the attraction. All their family members cheated with my presence. For the last three days, I was under the guidance of their superior. What I eat, where I sleep, when to go, and how to respect others. Every member of his family monitors everything. I felt as if I was computerized and instructed by others.

That was the day for...which I had been waiting for a long time. It's not mine... It happened to everyone's life. This night is unique for everyone. The special day made me feel excited. This was my reception date. A grand celebration happened there. All my inlaws, family members, and relatives came to that party. They all met with me, and the seniors were blessed with some tokens of love. I got a lot of ornamental gifts. I noticed that my husband was not looking at me among the crowd. Even not caring for me like a newly married couple behaves.

As the evening increases to the night. The crowd became thin. I went to my bedroom. The room flowered with flamboyance. After some time, he entered the room. I was trembling with fear. My body sweated out. He came and touched me.

Under the moon's soft silver glow, our twin hearts united in the sacred night. I lose myself in his eyes—an ocean of love reflecting the stars. Tight hugs and kisses fill the romantic atmosphere as we share dreams and desires. We felt solace in each other's chests. Mercury light fluttering shadows of passion to our atmospheric melody. Midnight kisses and tight hugs magnate our promises of celestial love and endless devotion. That honeymoon night, we embarked on a journey of boundless romance, a heart-to-heart forever entwined.

He became so romantic—still no difference between us. I did not feel a new erotic expression from him. After all, we enjoyed the whole night by caring and sharing. I asked him why he was making a difference to me. He became silent. I didn't ask anymore. Suddenly, the light switched off. You know how afraid I am of deep darkness.

***

Yes, that deep black night makes me horrible. I ran away to save my life. Three notorious and antisocial men ran behind me to rape me. Ugly night breathes like an enigmatic symphony of nocturnal life and pin-drop silence. My feet speed more than endanger, dear. Because some barking dog was running behind me. I try to save my life from them.

Finally, I ran into a lady standing near the national highway. She was very tall and healthy from what I guess from the running vehicle light. Suddenly, that lady turned back. Gave a smile. I felt... She might be safe. Those sex-hungry people running behind me stand by one side. Looking at me, they laughed and laughed. One of them said don't..worry, friend; here we are running behind a woman, but God has gifted two ladies for us. Let's go and enjoy ourselves.

Suddenly, like that, a lady stood like a mountain obstacle to them and shouted at them.

Hey..!...what do you want? Why are you falling behind that lady?

One of them said we want to satisfy our sexual desire.

Ok... I will arrange for you all.

I was getting afraid and cried. She assured me not to worry. I am safe there. Suddenly, she called all the girls. Four girls came from the backside of a banyan tree near the crop field. Again, she told them...girls...! They need satisfaction and happiness. Suddenly, all the girls arrived and took them to the crop field. After some time, those antisocial people came up with a tired face. Both were ready to go. Immediately, that lady said –Hello..where are you going? Who will pay money for better sexual satisfaction?

They refused to pay. All the women went there to catch those boys and beat them. They took all the money from them by searching their pockets. After some time, they left. I did not understand what was happening there. I was standing there with confidence. I was unable to understand what was happening to me. Why did I face all these things? Suddenly, that lady turned towards me and told me –sister ..." Don't worry... We have cleared all your obstacles, and you can go safely now.

Where will I go? I asked.

Your home.

It is such a deep darkness, and no one is there. Luckily, you saved me. I never feel ...I may be safe after some steps ahead.

But we can't save you later on. Why did you come here? Better go to your home. I will arrange some accommodation for you to drop by at your home.

Me –I have no home. My second husband forcefully gave me up.

She was astonished and asked me what was your intention.

Will you take me with you? I asked. Suddenly, she looked at me with a strange eye.

I think you have no idea who we are! We can't save you. Our life is drastic and chaotic. You can't come with us.

What's the problem with you? The first time, I faced a stranger whom I trusted a lot. That comes from the bottom of my heart. Many known people treat me as unknown. The first time, I trusted some female species who are more dangerous than males, which the public felt. I was going to blend with them.

But you don't know... We are prostitutes, and we are highly rejected by society but accepted by many dejected lovers, rejected husbands, and some sex hunger.

I was suddenly afraid and went back a step. Again, she said, "I know you will think about our feelings. We are prostitutes by chance, not by choice. Why did you come with us? Better return to your life from where you are.

I said —all my roads are closed. Will you give shelter? I have no faith in including my family members.

After listening to them, they all agreed to take me with them. After some time, an Andhra truck reached there. They were all sitting there. I also went with them. That truck ran towards the border. I asked that lady where are you going? She told me —we were going to Kolkata. Do you have any problems? We have no issues. If you want to go down...you may. The choice is yours.

Me: Beggars have no choice. I fully surrendered under your blessings. Because you saved my life. Today, I luckily escaped from my second husband. I was going to be murdered by their family members. While coming on the way, some people tried to trap me. You saved my life. So you are not my God but my Good friend. I am not thinking where you belong. What you are doing, that is your profession. I have no problems. Will you save me from evil society? My belongings suffocated me.

After listening to everything, she said, "If you are comfortable with us, then I have no problems. We will send you and settle in the right place.

I asked her what's...your name. I am Latike.

Again, she asked if she was worried about me and my autobiography. Keep patience.

Part 5

Oh ...sorry...I forgot that I am writing a letter to you. I must be confused about why I twisted my story. Because I was in my honeymoon bedroom and why I am talking about the story of a prostitute. Yes, there is a long gap between me, my life, and my family. Many times, my life comes with many twists. That was the day they kidnapped me with my knowledge and concern. I don't know why they accepted their offer. Yes...there's a lot of history I cleaned.

I assisted, and they assisted me, helped me to take with them. I went to the truck. The truck started its journey towards the city of Kolkata. I sat with their team. The first time, they kidnapped me with my concern. While on that journey, the truck driver asked and looked at me.

Queen... Where did you get such a lovely item? Will you give me a chance? To chase...oh...nice. One short.

I can't understand. Suddenly, I was getting afraid. She assured me. She said... −Ohh !...concentrate on driving. Don't look here and there. Otherwise, we will kick you. Nothing happens ...we will all die.

Suddenly, the driver said nothing would happen... if you were to die, is there anyone to cry? If something happens to me... it means if I die, my wife and family members will cry. But who will cry for you all?

One lady came and slapped that driver, Bastard..you know... we are orphans only for you all. We need not expect anyone's help. We are self-sufficient to manage ourselves.

The driver became silent and continued his driving. Really, on that night, I felt they were also like me, and everyone had a different story from mine. But why do they come here? What is the purpose? Many questions arise in my mind. I think I will ask them about their journey.

I did not get the opportunity to ask. All were busy chitchatting with the driver and themselves. But no one misbehaved with me. Sometimes, that naughty driver raises his hand towards them and touches their private part. Sometimes, they kiss each other. Still, no one opposes them. I was feeling uncomfortable. After some time, I fell into a deep sleep. Rough and plane roads changed my comfort zone. Still, I snuggled myself. Suddenly, I was woken up by a speed break by the driver. I saw the first sunshine with a clear sky. Crowds gradually increased— many vehicles and the public ran with their assignment. No one has time to stay. I got out of the truck and followed them. I walked with them. It was a curved road like a black snake. Suddenly, I asked them by breaking my introspective thoughts.

Hello..guys..where are you taking me? Where are you going?

One of them said ...don't worry... come with them. They will not kill me.

Without clarifying me, they keep on walking. I follow them. After some time, I reached their destination—a small BHK room with an attached washroom. I entered the room of that lady. She told me to sit on her bed. I sit on her bed and spread my body again in a sleeping posture.

I was getting tired. I was never alive the whole night before, even on my honeymoon night. After coming from the washroom, a lady came and sat near me. Combining my hair on her finger.

I felt concerned. With a hungry eye again, I asked – what's your name ...sister.

Calling me sister...that's sufficient. Why do you need to know my name? Everyone calls me by the same word. You may call this.

Still, I want your name. Whenever required, I may be safe by saying your name.

Yes... I am Patralekha. Now I am a dangerous brand of red light area. Endanger the lives of others. Everyone knows me as queen. Could you not ask anything about my past? I am living with my present. The whole night, I was tired. I have no patience to discuss a single word. If you look through my biography, you will find many stories. I spent many nights with a lot of experience. In my diary, many clients write autographs belonging to corporate heads, sales executives, and bastard police officers. It's a hobby that I have kept up with all night. Ohh !...my God. I can't say anymore. Could you give me a pleasant night's sleep without a dream?

Slowly..slowly... Patralekha went into deep sleep. I was still alive and alone. I walked and lay down near the window. Looking across the window towards the road. They are all busy running life and nonlife things doing their duty. It's just going to be ten o'clock. Children go to school. Laborers were working to demolish the building. Professionals were ready to do their job with a schedule. Yes..., everything is moving except me. I was sitting alone, a stagnant stone, thinking about what to do. Where will I go? Who will take care of me? I saw Patralekha already in a deep sleep. That night, she helped me and escaped from them. I was very anxious to know about Patralekha. I remembered ..., just a few minutes before she told me about her diary. I will go through her diary. I searched here and there. I got it from one corner of myself. By taking it, I went through that dairy. I was astonished by what a life she has! It was written as:

Hi..I am Patralekha. Highly ostracised, discriminated against, humiliated, and exploited with time and tides. Now, I am the queen of this area. It's the achievement of my life or detachment from society. I made a mistake, or it's my misfortune. It's a mistake or blunder. A lot of corporations seek my help to accomplish their business. Yes, I am Patralekha, a spy for corporate success. Everyone expects my presence to clinch business secrecy from their rivalry. Yes, I got ample rewards and recognition by giving my plethoric pleasure and sexual satisfaction. By the way, I am highly respected by many corporate clients on the back side of corporate success.

I am Patralekh, a classical dancer who became the heroine of this industry. You may detest or hate my personality. But my presence is the same as your mother, sister, and daughter's many lives. Prostitutes like me protect the life of the female species from the exploiting, intimidating, and victimizing eyes of sex hunger. My alluring eyes protect them from many scandals like rape, murder, and sexual harassment. What can I do more, and what can a country expect from a rural village girl doing?

A meta-analysis conducted in 2009 totaled sixty-five case studies in twenty-two countries. From that impression of the "overall world figure." The main findings of the study were

Approximately 19.7% of girls generally face sexual abuse below the age of eighteen years. If I collect a lot of data, it will be a separate volume book. My dairy has no such space. Why was I running behind such a carrier? A girl from a poor rural family never dreams about a bright future. So the consequence is my life. A slum queen of the redlight area. Where people and police are tortured every moment if we are unable to satisfy them. Why is prostitution not legalized in India? At least, we save our savings from police and hackers.

My life biography started in Rajapore in the Murshidabad district of West Bengal. I belong to the very poor below the poverty line, having a widowed mother and one little sister. I did well in my primary school studies but was excellent at dancing. The alluring eyes of my school dance teacher abused me. He assured me that to overcome the poverty and starvation of my family, I would have to go dancing as a career and go for dance programs in different places. I agreed with my teacher and went with him at fourteen. She took me to stage shows, reality shows, and dance programs at corporate festivals. I stayed with him in many hotels and resorts. He was exploiting me both sexually and mentally. What I earned, he was taking seventy percent as commission in the name of expenses and expenditures on me. I was hopeless and had no words to say.

Yes... I remember that night. The dance program finished around eleven. I stayed with my dance teacher. I got four hundred rupees.

He demanded all the money. I said it is essential for the bread and butter of my family. I can't give you. Suddenly, he told me he had spent much time on my growth and performance. I am what is only for him. I honored his voice and told him I had given my fees before. That month was highly essential for my family's expenses. My mother was suffering from a chronic disease and had my schooling fees, I had to pay. She agreed and offered to present my body for the whole night as teachers' fees, which is gurudakshina (fees). My family's financial liability and scarcity matter to me.

On the other hand, my teachers' sexual desire. In that hotel, she forcefully raped me more than two times. I opposed it but failed to protect myself. I have never seen such notorious activities of such a scoundrel teacher. Such teachers are the black curse of a noble profession. After coming home, I told my mother not to participate in any dance program. My mother agreed with my statement. But I had no other way of earning money for my family's daily expenses. A village consists of poor households.

Daily earnings never continue for the next few days. No one raised their helping hand for my family. So I was helpless.

So I went to my teacher's house and accepted all his terms and conditions. Again, I started my journey with the help of my sir. I somehow manage my family and my studies. One day, my teacher asked about my future and invited me to Calcutta. A national dance program was going to be arranged at Victoria Memorial Hall. I agreed with him. It was a seven-day cultural function. I went with my dance teacher. Stayed with him in a hotel near Howrah station. A small cottagelike room is there. During that seven-day function, one day, my Sir told me that he had spoiled my life. He realized a lot and cried. Finally, Sir told me to fulfill the loss of my life and chastity; he will be my life partner forever. I agree, as Sir is saying. With my impure body and vituperate mind, I will offer my celestial love to my husband. Better I accepted my teacher's word and took him as my husband. So I will have remorse forever.

Again, ignited with new hope and received my teacher as my husband. In the seven-day cultural program, I did well. Rewarded with many cash prices. All my competitors were from different corners of the state. I secured the 6th position in that program. I trust my teacher.

On the 4th day, my teacher told me: Patralekha ... You will go for a whole night dance program. Keep all your money. Kolkata is not a safe place. There may be a chance of losing your bag. Who is here near and dear without me? If anyone stole your bag, then what would you do?

I trusted his word, gave all my bags to him, and attended the program. In that valediction program, I enjoyed and performed at the best level because that program appeared to me as an opportunity in the film industry. The selected top ten will get an entry pass to the Kolkata film industry. I dreamed of a lot of success. The program finished at 12.30 at night. The crowd gradually became thin. Sir came to me and told Patralekha it was already very late. The hotel is closed. Late-night entry is not permitted.

Patralekha sir..., where will we go? I don't know. I am new to this Kolkata town.

Sir, Don't worry...I am with you. You are my wife. I will take care of you and look after all your needs. Here is one of my relatives' houses at Sova Bazar. We will go and stay there. Tomorrow morning, we will go to Murshidabad.

I agreed with my sir's voice, and his confidence compelled me to go to his relative's house. It was midnight. I was trembling with fear. The area was calm and quiet. Some notorious people came to that house, and some went out. I feel something different.

I said, "Sir... it's not a good place. We should leave that place. I am not feeling comfortable here.

Why are you afraid? It's my relative's house. Nothing will happen. My aunt is a social worker. For some purpose, people come from different places. It's a rest house for everyone.

I trust my sir... sorry, my future husband, and go with him. Every room was closed. Two to three women were wandering near the corridor. By looking at me, one of them smiles with a satirical look. I did not care. Sir, take me to a room. We both stayed there. It was 2 o'clock. Looking at the bed, I felt sleepy. I said, Sir," I am getting tired; I want to sleep."

Slowly, I stretched my body and lay down on the bed. Suddenly, Sir came to me and slept on me. I was not uncomfortable with him. Because I accepted him as my husband, Sir asked me for permission to move forward. Today is our honeymoon night. We enjoyed the whole night. No one is here to disturb us. I also agree with him. We enjoyed ourselves underneath the blue-golden zero light.

We feel the actual moonlight falling on us. He kissed me, and I also. That atmosphere became a sonnet of bliss and testament to the depth of our eternal kiss. Both of our bodies merged with celestial fire and ablaze with desired passion. My husband touched me with different sensational parts of my body. Both our erotic expressions and celestial feelings achieve an optimum level of heavenly happiness.

—◇—

Part 6

I don't know when I slept last night. Slowly, I woke up. By closing my eyes, I raised my hand to the other side of my bed. I felt no one was there. Suddenly, I was astonished and got up from bed. I saw no one was there. Where is Sir? I opened the door. It was locked from the outside. I knocked several times, but there was still no response from outside. Immediately, I shouted inside the room –help ...me...please help me.

Suddenly, a sound came from the opposite side of the door.

Who is shouting? You are sold to us. Don't shout.Doont...s..h..o..u...ttt.!

Who is that bloody nonsense? I shouted in a loud voice.

Suddenly, the door opened. I saw a fat lady with a giant look enter the room and slap me. And told me not to shout. My sir has sold me here. This place is Sonagchhi. Here, the fleshes are sold at different prices. You are a valuable asset to this Kothi (empire). You have to satisfy all the needs of the customer. We will earn ample rupees. I was getting afraid and trembled with fear. I oppose that fat lady. I said," Please leave me. I am not this type of girl. Please don't destroy my celestial beauty and chastity. I am requesting you ...please help me. I will go with my dance teacher. Where is he?

Suddenly that lady told me, Oh...your dance teacher... Malay. He is our prime agent. He sells you here for three lakh rupees.

No, it's impossible. I loved him very much. I can't forget him.

She laughed and said: "What, What to forget?" Already forgotten at the cost of money. You are our revenue-generating asset. We invested three lakhs. You pay double the amount, which means six lakhs. After you leave,

I perform a dance program for three hundred rupees. Three lakhs is like the sky and has no limit to where I get. Who will save me? Suddenly, that lady called me and warned me that if I agreed with their condition, nothing would be impossible, as you might think.

I was strict with my voice and refused the offer. Suddenly, she called a Sardar.

He came with a leather belt. Entered like a roaring tiger. With that belt, he whipped me incessantly. I cried and cried. No one was there to help me. From the bottom of my heart, my innocent eyes and emotions have no value to others. Immediately, two girls were forcefully thrown into the room. Incessantly, we were all bitten by that sardar for thirty minutes. Our bodies were sketched with straight red and curved lines on that belt. The geography of my body has already changed. We were all dressed out. The first time, I was with a naked body in front of an indoor audience. Everyone enjoyed the naked geography of our lives. That lady tightened my long hair and warned me I would be safe if I agreed with her conditions.

I had been hungry for the last two days and was bitten by them hourly.

The other two girls were very innocent. I asked them what happened to them. Why did they get here, and why?

One of them told them notorious agents trapped them. One girl was from a Hindu community. She belongs to the Tamil Brahmin community. She fell in love with a Muslim boy. The concept of love jihad was intensely immersed in the inertia of the mind. I have heard many cases, like the Kerala story and the Kashmir Files, where girls were tortured and trapped by an antisocial, terrorist religion. But the soft side of religion has no value on the foolish public biased by regional and political agendas. With the increase in TRP, the media highlights all these issues. But no one cares about our shadowy story of burning candles and rotten flowers like such black roses. Yes, those red roses were converted into black roses due to poverty, starvation, family liability, and trust in a bastard lover.

The next day, I woke up from bed with the voice of a

crying lady. I was suffering from hunger and getting thirsty. My washroom water connection was locked. For the last two days, I have been hungry like anything. Still, I was so audacious with my decision. After several times, I saw that the Tamil girl agreed with their terms and conditions. So they took her to another room. And warm treatment from that morning. I know she was forcefully doing that nasty work. Her ethics, thoughts, and noble purpose were demolished with a piece of bread and a cup of butter. For the last three days, I was on a hunger strike. They forced me to obey their rules. A gain with a piece of burning cigarette pushed into my lap. I was unable to resist such torture. The end of the panic made me senseless. I don't know. What happened to me? After several hours, I found myself in the bed of that lady who had been torturing me for the last few days. She was combing my hair. Some medicine was kept near that bed. An old retired doctor was discussing with her. After some time, he left that corridor. I tried to wake up. I felt some internal pain from postintercourse activities. I need the help of someone. No one was coming to me. I need the help of that lady. She assured me nothing would happen. You take one week's rest. Suddenly, I asked what happened. Why should I take a rest? What happened to me? Who are you? Why are you forcing me to use the nasty policy?

Quickly, she smiled and said I am Leela. I am your Leela Anty. This is Leela Sagar. All satisfied and dissatisfied pilgrims come to this place for their celestial harmony. I can't destroy their celibacy only for some respondents like you. You are here for my business.

You are strongly determined about your chastity. Ok. That is noble but not sustainable.

I was astonished. Something had happened to me. Why are my internal organs not in a normal condition? I shouted and asked them what had happened to me and why they were playing with my sentiments.

Leela: Oh..! stop. Don't shout. It's not good for your health. Already, four young and dynamic boys enjoyed your body. The first time, without your willingness, I generated thirty thousand five hundred—a good income from the first day. No one of my subjects generated such revenue. Tiring condition, you satisfied everyone very generously. Why shouldn't you try to complete the target of three lakhs of revenue I expect from you? And you will be free forever.

As you sow, so you reap.

I realized from that day that Leela Aunty's behavior had changed. She identified me as a catalyst for her recurring income. She has tried investment from that day to till date. For the last seven days, I have been lying in bed and taking my breakfast, lunch, and dinner to the same place. Every moment was excruciating for me. Many meetings were conducted in that corridor. Leela Aunty was sitting near to me. It is in her court where many discussions have happened.

On Day One, a political leader came to meet Leela. He was asking about the development of that colony. Leela gave some proposals for the development of society. Prostitutes were downstroke and backward people. They need some legal rights. I shucked what they needed. What are the legal rights they need in illegal activities? I have no such idea about this Sonagachi colony. Political aspirants use more than twenty thousand vote banks.

They played a vital role in changing the vote during the upcoming election. So political leaders come here to spend their time not for sexual desire but for their political motive. So they are the career-changing and twist point for their life.

On the second day, I saw some company agent come to Leela's house. One of them was a private company manager. They need some young girls to participate in their cocktail party. Their superior and boss were coming to Kolkata for a corporate audit. To satisfy them, the company provides entertainment. So, there is nothing wrong with love, war, and sex.

On the third day, I was astonished that some NGO leaders were coming to meet Leela Anti. Their main agenda was to eradicate AIDS from society. It was an international Non-governmental organization. They got a lot of funding from abroad. Yes, people are providing their excess income, black money, and under-table income to these NGOs and enjoying tax benefits. It is a source of income for

NGOs to manage such activities, like different campaigns, game activities, rallies, inauguration, and ceremony activities. They also provide condoms, sanitary pads, and some antipregnancy tablets. All raising their hand for service to humanity is service to God. But no one helps to settle their life with a prostitute. No one showed their interest in taking a prostitute as a family member. We are the scapegoat for everyone's success. All are showing their sympathetic hand to fulfill their purpose.

On Fourth Day, I saw some police officers come to that house. Two-star and three-star officers went to the picture of my unseen eyes. A few of them discuss their percentage with stupid Leela. Three constables entered the room with three sex workers. They came after thirty minutes. All were coming with smiling faces. After some discussion, they took their commission and left the place. I saw the first time the police took a commission for illegal work. It's their outside income apart from salary.

That day, I saw some agents coming there to take their pending amount and supply girls. Some Sardar were there who were protecting that Sonagachi area. Generally, every fifth is Friday. There is internal payment for everyone. Friday evening is bustling. Weekend time is crucial for everyone. Everyone comes to this area for their refreshment. They are all waiting to garner business by offering such girls.

Saturday and Sunday, the flow of the public from

different corners of the country is excellent. A maximum number of tourists came to Sonagachi. Here, some girls are at a high rate and attend luxury hotels. Looking at all these scenarios within seven days, I sucked how this society is running like sex with seduction. The regular public strictly abandons sex city civilization. Society is fully covered with safety, security, self-esteem, and respect. We are the best complement for those respected dignitaries. They never care about us, either. But when they feel any erectile dysfunction from their life partner. They need us as their bed partner. Slowly, my mind changed or deteriorated with these nasty fragrances of culture. I was forced to do it and was deeply involved in overcoming these slum areas. In my unconscious mind, I was napped several times by an unknown person. As I belonged to a destitute family, I was firm with immunity. I recovered from internal pain and body aches without the use of antibiotics.

One day, Leela Aunty called me in a soft voice.

Leela: Listen Patralekha... You are in the Red light area. If you try, nobody will escape. Better you polish or perish forever. Everyone comes to these areas at a oneway entrance. No exit door is here. If you try to leave..you can't. Everyone has such a black background. Who will save you and why? This is a different industry that continued from English civilization before independence. Many come, many go. Who cares? Many lives were destroyed. Who agrees that they enjoy a luxurious life with colorful evenings?

Yes... a great writer, Taslima Nasrin, said *if you do not protect rape, which is not under your control...better you enjoy it.*

Patralekha: I am not here to enjoy such slums. I want to grow up with a better future. I want to leave this place.

Leela: Onesided your death. Where no one will cry. On the other hand, your willingness. The choice is yours.

One person came with delicious food with an aromatic fragrance coming out. That smell tempted me. My hunger level was at its peak. I was unable to control it. Eat all the food. Nonveg items were delicious. He gave good food to me to garner business. I was strict with my decision. But I don't know if some molecule was added to my food. They hypnotized me. What they instructed, I did without hesitation. Gradually, I was in their race to attract clients. Every day, what I earned was deducted from my target amount. When I was suffering from an illness or any disease, they spent money on my good health. But my debit and credit account always has a negative balance. Sometimes, Leela's aunt sends some money to my home with the help of my school teacher. They told me I was working in Kolkata. I packed with many assignments. When my office gives me time, I will come to meet my mother.

Listening to these made me happy that I was contributing something to my family. They will not be hungry any longer. I spent many colorful, torturing nights with different sex partners who have studied the geography of my body.

xxx   xxx

A little tear comes out from the corner of my eyes. I realize how Patralekha lived life. If I compare this Latika's life path, it is far better than Patralekha's. Suddenly, a dairy was snatched from my hand. I turned back. No one was there. Patralekha is standing behind me. I was afraid. Without anyone's permission, it's not fair to involve one's dairy. I said sorry, sister...I was feeling bored. As time passed, I went through your biography. Sorry ... your dairy. Please ..don't mind. I apologize for my unknowing mistake.

Patralekha: It's ...OK. You should not go through my dairy. It's not my dairy. It's a breaking life story that I kept secret. You should not reread it because you may have made the wrong impression on me. It's a story from the last twenty years. I have been living here for the last eighteen years.

Me: Will the same situation continue with me? Whether they will make my life hell. As I have no option, I trust you...and come with you.

Patralekha: (Laughed)Don't worry... I am with you. No one will touch you. This situation is not now. Everything has changed. Here, sex is a profession. Today, I will drop you off at a charitable organization. There you will be safe forever. You leave with your new life.

Me: If you don't mind, shall I ask one question?

OK, tell me without any hesitation. –Patralekha said.

Again, I asked what happened to you? Why is your life so hectic? Is it the true story of your life? Why are you showing sympathy for me?

Patralekha: Yes... don't worry. I will tell you all this. Keep patience. Let's come with me and grab lunch. Everything you know. Let's have a walk...time will solve the situation.

I went outside. I was walking, followed by Patralekha. It was just 1 o'clock. When I went with her, some people were looking at me from a different angle. Some people comment on me. But didn't care.

Well, come to Sonagachi.

How are you, darling?

Are you free..... for..... me......, tonight?

Many things listen. I was silent but trembled with anger.

Patralekha went to the STD booth and called someone. I was waiting outside and heard some murmuring sounds. She was discussing something about me. After some time, she came out, and we had lunch there. I got a packed lunch as she ordered. I don't know why Patralekha (sister) watched my way of eating. I asked her

What happened? Why are you looking at me?

no...no... I am not looking at what and how much you are eating. I am studying how your hunger positioned you in such a pathetic position. We are all running behind on food. It may be someone's belly satisfaction or beneath belly satisfaction. Every time, female species are treated as food for others. From Mahavarat and Ramayana ...everywhere, women are tortured by a male-dominated society. The same thing is happening in our red-light area. We present ourselves by feeding others as food. Our clients come to us by purchasing food instead of money from us. With that money, we purchase food here. So money is not everything. Without money, you can't buy anything. But is the process or medium of earning money genuine or not?

Are you thinking ... It's ethical? The way you earned it!

Yes, it's true. Nobody wants to walk this way. I am a prostitute, not by choice but by chance. You may think it's a job, a curse, or a sin. So everybody hates to neglect us.

Will you force me to do what happened in your life?

No... My dreams and thoughts are different. With due deference, I positioned you on the royal and real stage. Where you build the rest of your life systematically, no one will come to meet you. Disturb you.

What do you mean...sister?

Wait a while...a person will come. You will go with

him. He will take you to that NGO. They will teach and guide you how to live. That organization is working for the eradication of AIDS, child labor, and education. A few months ago, I associated with them. Their noble thoughts impressed me. They also took my interview and published it in the national newspaper. We also fight for justice.

In such illegal work, what justice do you need? Who will protect you? Everyone will laugh at you. Because no one will support prostitution, and it should be legalized.

I do not support or encourage prostitution. Those who are on this line in their lives should be comfortable. None of this society accepts our culture. If we leave, no one will give us a job and invite us as their family member if the govt approves Prostitution as a legal profession. We can earn money. No agent will drag our cash. Many times, the police threatened us by imposing rules and regulations. They are great commission agents and security providers. What we paid by selling our naked bodies, many times they charged a fifty percent commission daily earning. Once upon a time, I was queen in this red-light area. I was paid the highest amount among all sex workers. Many documentary films are produced here to change the mindset of the public. People also like the flow of wind. They are supporting us and increasing the sales volume of the film and media industry, TRP, and the goodwill of political leaders. No one gives justice to us. OK, it's not the right place to discuss this.

We had already finished our lunch. Street food has a unique test in the city of Kolkata. Many street vendors manage their families from this business. Sonagachi is also known as Sovabazar. The Aristocrat family never told Sonagachi about the place. It's a curse or sin ...I don't know. I went to the Sovabazar metro with Patralekha. We were waiting for someone to take me to settle into my life. I asked Patralekha.

Didi..., May I ask something, if you don't mind?

Patralekha told me –No... Problem: you asked what was coming to your mind.

What happened to that teacher? Have you met him later? How is your family member taking care of them after you leave? I hoped you wouldn't ask me why I went through your dairy.

I am leaving you today. Why are you so sympathetic to me? I have never seen such a benevolent lady in my life.

Patralekha told me Don't worry... I will tell you everything. Let the perfect time come. However, time and tides wait for none. But time will answer.

We had already reached the Sovabazar metro station. One person was waiting for both of us. Patralekha introduced me to that person. After some time, I departed from Patralekha.

———◇———

Part 7

It was quarter to five. I reached the NGO office. I found out that the organization is a charitable trust. It works for poor, destitute, and downtrodden children, along with orphan parents who have enjoyed a luxurious aristocratic family life. I wait at their reception counter. That attendant took me to that room. Some dignitaries were sitting there. They asked some formal verbal questions and entered my name on the register. They offered me some new clothes. I allotted a Dermidorylike room. Some older women, orphan children, and two women were there. I was new to this place. All are looking at me as if I came from another planet. One older adult asked me in Bengali. Where did I come from? Why did I join? What is the problem with me? I said, "Nothing happened to me. I just came here on the recommendation of my sister."

Another older adult just told me you are fortunate. You are not unfortunate like us.

I did not say anything. I know how unfortunate my life is. It was 8 p.m. All were ready for dinner. I went to a dinner party hall with other boarders. That dining table is full of delicious food I had never seen. I had a full belly meal. There was no restriction on taking a diet. I saw how people ate their food very happily. I thought, why didn't I get to this destination before? This is a very calm and peaceful place. There is no scarcity of bread, butter, water, relationships, fellow feelings, and belongingness. They all provide me with a warm carpet. I never felt any lack on that night. I go into a deep, cold sleep without tension. The following day, at 5 o'clock, I got up from bed. All are ready to go to the prayer room. I also followed the same rules and schedule. After prayer, they all did some smooth meditation and little exercises. Then, everyone went to the washroom. I also did my daily morning routine. Immediately, I heard a loud and melodious song. Suddenly, I went to the meeting hall. Oh..! What an excellent scene. It is such a colorful arrangement I have never seen before.

All are greeting one older person with happy birthday wishes. I went near that older man who told me how fortunate I am! I wish him a happy birthday. He blessed me. But I am not so lucky as to accept his blessings. The cake-cutting ceremony was full of enjoyment. A breakfast was also provided for all in that ceremony hall. Everyone greeted me as a new guest. I told him I was not a guest. You treat me as your family member. On that day, I was delighted. I thought this was the best day of my life. I have never had this type of regard before. Even my maternal family and mother–in–law's family. After that celebration, they all went to their assigned jobs, like gardening work, tailoring, dancing, teaching children, carpentry, and watching movies. Here, all types of job facilities are provided to entertain their life. No one is here to work forcefully. Each one is helping the other as per their core competency.

I was roaming here and there. A lovely garden, veranda, and long road designed with attractive wall paintings was mindblowing. I was roaming as a traveler. The gorgeous roses in that garden attract me. So, my forced emotion dragged me into the garden. There are not only different colored roses but also other attractive flowers. It looks like a botanical garden. I saw all the flowers' fragrance and emotional appeal, which attracted me a lot. I became an environmental lover and spent some time with them. While walking in between the trees, I saw an older man sitting beneath the tree. I was astonished...What happened to that stranger? Why is he beneath the shadow of that tree? Slowly, slowly, I walked and reached there.

Alash!.. how strange... That older man is nothing unknown to me. He is that grandpa who was celebrating his 76th birthday this morning. He was happy. Why is he sitting alone? I just called him:

Dadu...(Grandfather)what happened to you ..why are you sitting alone?

He turned his face. I saw some unbelievable tears coming from both the corners of his eyes. His sorry figure strangled me. Keeping emotion aside, I asked: what happened, Dadu? Aren't you happy? Why sit alone and cry?

Do you think I am crying?

Then what...!

It's a tear of realization, a tear of self-introspection. I examined myself...what blunder I made.

I can't get you, Dadu. You were happy in the morning. You enjoyed your birthday party. But why... Such incessant flowing tears? What do you mean to say? Aren't you glad about staying here?

No.., at all. Here, no one is happy. We are all here, not by choice. I am enjoying life like the solitude of Alexander. If I had wings, I would have crossed heaven.

Then..why was the celebration function just a few hours ago? It's not about your willingness. Then why do you stay here? Leave the place and go with your family for the rest of your life.

That is my bad luck. I have a family, but I am alone. My son is staying abroad with his family. A few months ago, my wife passed away. For her (wife) funeral ceremony, they came here and told me to go abroad with them. I refused their offer. I am very nostalgic. I don't like to spend my life in a metropolitan city. Apartment life kills me. So they told me to stay there without my interest. I think my retired life should be in my duplex home, with a garden in front of it. My wife would have sat in the garden and spent time with a cup of tea. Everything spoiled within a short period.

You call your son, or you may stay alone with the help of a paid servant. There is no need to go there. You get a better retired old life. At least you die in peace.

You call your son, or you may stay alone with the help of a paid servant.

That is not possible. My son agreed with this NGO. They will take care of the rest of my life instead of giving me purchase land. I spent my lifetime income on his career. He settled abroad. Learn their culture. Applied to me. Keeping me in an old age house. For half of my lifetime income, I build a lovely home that is sold to a builder. This NGO will take care till death, which I never expected from my next generation. You will be astonished at where I am sitting in my land. The garden is also my property.

So, this NGO is occupying your land forcefully. So why not file a case against them?

With whom I will fight. Who will support me? How long will I live?

NGOs are known as Non-governmental organizations. Somehow, they are showing as a charitable organization. Behind the word charity, they cheated their organization. Ruined the life of the poor destitute. You have not seen their pseudo teeth, which are more dangerous. All NGOs are not like this. To whom I will say the truth. Some corrupt Government Officers became a helping hand for them. Better you leave this place. Otherwise, you will perish if you do not polish with their rule and regulations. Obeying their authority, I am spending the rest of my life rationing out my pain also.

I could not digest their thoughts and culture toward such a noble organization. I somehow manage to listen and stand with that older man. After some time, one attendant came to that place and threatened Dadu.

What are you doing here? In the last hour, we searched for you everywhere. What you told her. Come ...come.

The attendant put a slabbed on his cheek and bitten. I try to oppose that person. He told me that he was mentally distressed. Don't worry, we'll take care.

They took that older man by whipping him. I was helpless to protect that innocent and phlegm mind. I think their life is more miserable than my life.

Such life in this world is so pathetic. Many struggles are spoiled with time and tides. Who cares about the lives of others? All are running for their profit, growth, and improvement. I don't think the rest of my lifespan will run smoothly. Still, I am not in a position to judge anyone. I was standing in the middle of a rose garden. All flowers throw an ambiguous look with their fragrance. I did not stay there for more than a second.

By the way, I spent the day having some bitter and better experiences. Many programs happened on that day. Went to sleep. I was lying on the bed with a living anesthetic body. I don't know. Why, that night, I remembered my near and dear. I have seen the innocent eyes of my family members. I don't know what and where my family is! When they need my presence. I am feeling their absence. If Patralekha is staying alone and far away from their near and dear..so wasn't I?

I have never thought about my near and dear, but I think about my near belongings. The whole night, I couldn't get a good sleep. I was thinking about the innocent older man. Many of them...but no one is here. I am alone except for patralekha, but I think about the consequences of my life. I slowly ...slowly went into a deep dream.

It was a beautiful morning. I woke up from bed stretching and enlarging my body posture with closed eyes. Wash my face again and again. I felt my body with some unknown pain. I unrecognized that pain. After I entered the washroom, I showered and bathed in cold water. When I spread my hand in my different private areas. I felt vaginal pain with dry blood coming out of my body. I carefully and consciously bathed and came out with my new dress.

I told the hostel warden about my illness. She gave me a confused smile and took me to the nurse's room. There, one young doctor was prescribing many prescriptions. I went in that queue to reach that doctor. The doctor asked for some signs and symptoms of my body. He gave me some painkillers and ointment to use my vaginal area. I was astonished ……, what happened to me? Why I felt the same weakness after my 1st honeymoon. I ignored that pain with my deep involvement and interaction with others. I liked that place. Gathered all generations of people with their different activities. I went to another building, the Golden Children's Hub.

Where all sweet kids, teenage boys, and girls were kept, and almost all the kids were orphans. They lived here with bread and butter—carefree children wandering here and there. I went there and spent some time with them. Really... I realized how their life is. Without parents, they were enjoying their life with nature. Where the earth is their bed. The sky is the roof. Sometimes, the calm wind creates a blessing in the hands of a caring mother. I was fortunate to have my childhood with my beloved parents. My parents were very caring for me and my mistakes. So, I am never wayward like others. My life was so easy and smooth. Now, I feel their love, emotion, and belongingness converted into hate, detest, and bitterness. Is it the life of a human being? Why did we require a family? If the consequence is this!

I was comparing my life with those of the orphan children. They are better than me. In the future, they will never disheartened. From the beginning, they lost everything. What extra challenges nature gives. They learn to struggle from their birth to the end of life. One of them I took very carefully. She looked so sweet. By hugging her, I felt my motherhoodness. Yes, I know that dream never turns into truth. I have to live without love.

Is it impossible to live without love? That baby was kissing my cheek and, many times, beating on my face smoothly. I have no words to express her innocent love. I lovingly bit her little finger. She smiled. I spent some time with her. One lady came towards me and smiled at me. I had never seen her before. I reacted the same as she did. That young lady took that baby from me and walked a few steps. I also followed her. We both sat near a flat podium. She kept that child in her lap. Open her breast and started feeding. I was astonished and asked.

Are you her biological mother?

"Yes", she said. Her statement put me in a dilemma. How is it possible? Her mother was there when she was an orphan. Again, I asked –then ..., why are you staying here? You have no family.

Yes... Once upon a time, I had. But now I am alone.

So why are you here? Your inlaw's family tortured you, or you divorced like me.

No..., no. I have not married yet. I am a bachelor.

A lot of quirkiness was created in my mind. I eagerly

asked –if you don't mind ...may I ask about your past and present?

Why should I mind ......? – she said.

Then why are you here?

It's my wish. On the other hand, no option is there.

I asked –I couldn't understand what you were saying. Each statement creates confusion. Will you clear such a confusing story?

Before you found out about my story, what did you get?

Know ... I can't give you a solution, but my suggestion and emotional sharing could be better for both of us. I am new to my routine world, which is full of rules and regulations. I am suffocated at every step of life. Somehow, I got relaxed here. I think that organization is suitable for everyone. Each one always appreciates its noble work culture and philanthropic motive. How do you feel, Mam?

After listening to my literary words of expression, she laughed and became silent. After some time, she said," You know Shilpa Saha.

Yes, I know her very well, not by her face but by the news channel. She was raped by a director and tortured. By the way, she was a Bengali actor. But is there any relevance to this conversation? It was approximately two to three years in the news. Nothing is coming ... it means it is not a hot topic.

Yes ...once upon a time, that hot topic girl was sitting before you. I am that girl, Shilpa Saha.

I felt ashamed. Why was I asking and discussing this celebrity? I should not have said this type of statement. I closed my eyes and bowed my head. She smiled and asked why you felt shy. It's not your fault. Everyone is talking about me. When I was a celebrity and now in that situation. I had a great dream. I started my career with modeling. I also did well in my academic career.

But... I am not so talented. Therefore, my beloved avoided me, and their family members rejected me. –I said.

Again, the celebrity started her story because she was coming to the Kolkata film industry for a better future career.

She fell in love with a renowned director. Who was committed to being a life partner? Many actors and directors clinched their benefits by showing many dreams. She had no option but to avoid it. One day, she was interacting with a director. Her talent does not doubt to judge.

On the other hand, the director had a lot of dreams. She was very close to that person. The director also said that he was in love with her. If she cooperates, they will both work on a big project. She will also be married to him, and they will both be in the same industry.

I saw her eyes full of tears. I wiped out some running tears. She told me.

Don't try ...because a lot of tears will come. You can't dry that tear of the ocean full of pain and agony. I will not see that consequence if I am conscious of my future. I never denied his wish and interest. She loved me as she wished. But that was not love. Cheaters are never lovers. Many times, I was in a controversial situation. On my backside, people were talking about my foolishness. And praise in front of me. So, I could not recognize the exact horoscope because of my simple beliefs. That young director was an experienced cheater.

One morning, I sprang out of bed. Some uncommon vomiting happened. The director was slipping near to me. He called the doctor and told me I was sick. The doctor gave him advice, some medicine, and a few tests. After a few days, the report came. I was pregnant. It was not a secret camera. Everything flashes out with a lot of spicy news. In the competition to run TRP, I was a catalyst for everyone. Some people blame that young director. My close supporters left me to prove him as a glittering diamond. I was unable to recognize which was wrong and which was correct. So I was the loser. This NGO assured me of justice. So, they appointed a new advocate to fight against the director. Many producers supported that director. I fell in love and permitted him to have sex. The only reason was my true love for him. I never felt. It was my mistake. I have to judge the perfect person. Yes...the situation has changed.

Time and tides wait for none. Now, no one is getting behind that matter. I am not a hot cake for everyone's table. I trust this NGO, but they also played with me. Later, I learned that the owner of this NGO was a friend of that film producer. Through that network channel, I was bound to be silent. My baby is just two years old. You heard about me just three years ago.

Yes, I am unable to remember precisely. But you are right.

For my justice, legal matters are discussed at district-level court. The court is running with date and money. My hopes and expectations are paralyzed day by day.

I am getting helpless and hopeless. I never thought about killing the baby. Generally, girls are born with some emotion, sentiment, and attachment, and how I will be off that track. Still, I am hoping that my baby will get justice. The creator is not so cruel to their creation.

It was 2 PM. That baby was in deep sleep. Shilpa Mam took that baby to her bedroom. Before leaving me, she said we would talk later. My baby is dreaming about her father. I have many things ...but nothing. I will come to you and find out about you.

I stoned there. I saw many people with many pathetic stories. Some broken lives will never be built again. Still, with many hopes, people are living here. Sky the limits of all hopes. Why is life like burning hopes? No one is happy in the world, but everyone is behind happiness.

I went a step ahead again. There were other members I met. Her sorry figure created many doubts in my mind. I anxiously moved to her and asked how are you. Are you happy here like others?

Have you seen any person happy in this world? Means this premises. she replied.

I was in doubt. Why? I just casually asked. Her statements hurt me a little.

No.. I am not happy I replied.

Yes ..., I know you. Just two days before you come here to ration out your pain. But the truth is always truth. No one gives the perfect solution to your remedies. You are the panacea of all your remedies. By the way, I am an unknown name adding to your life. You don't try to get to know me better. I lost everything in my life. I am searching for peace. But this place is nothing. Wait for some days. You will learn many things.

She didn't say anything, but what she said put me in a state of confusion. I was not bothered by her statement. Likewise, many respondents I met there every day. Everyone is coming and going. Sometimes, dignitaries come with ample donations. NGOs' financial strength is increasing day by day. I don't know how they are helping the community. Service to God is service to humankind or service to their property. Gradually, I realized the horoscope of charitable organizations. Some borders incessantly work for this organization because their mind and bodies are ablaze with a patriotic and philanthropic flavor of using idle human resources in the name and fame of their NGO. So, after all, I have to be silent. I am not a leader to change the world. It is better to adjust myself according to the situation.

Yes... Pritam.., I can't tolerate it when it comes to me. After all, I have some bitter with better experiences of this society. I never opposed their progress and growth because they helped me during my time. Everything was beyond my patience.

One morning, when I woke up, I felt some pain in my abdomen. I went to the bathroom. Severe vomiting with headache. It was not due to my illness. Some pregnant tendencies I felt. I complain against trusty members. I called Patralekha. She also came. The doctor confirmed that I was pregnant. I shouted there. Some media reporters asked many questions about me. I went to the police station for an affair. I was happy that everything would flash out. I will spoil the goodwill and reputation of the NGO. Patralekha supports me a lot. I asked Patralekha why they played with my sentiments. I have no physical relationship with anyone.

Patralekha, I have no idea what is happening to you. I never left the culprit. I kept you here for your safety. That redlight area is better than this holistic place.

At that time, Shilpa came. She asked me," What do you do, Latika? You can't avenge your loss. I told you from day one. Be alert. They will use your chastity and sell at a high rate on the market. You are a scapegoat for all blame and curse. I have already made a complaint to the police

. But Shilpa refused. I was getting angry at Shilpa. Why is she denying me? What is her interest?

Why are you obstructing going forward? Silence is not the solution to my chastity.

Shilpa, What will you do? Upper-level people sell everyone. You told the media a few hours before. But it's not breaking news today. The police are silent and may issue any charge sheet against you.

On the other hand, you think if you blame the organization, they will be rejected, and no funds will come from different countries. Here, some people live with hope and belief. Once this NGO closes, you think about the consequences for dependent members. I know they are doing some malpractice and misusing power. But nowadays, NGOs are acting as a catalyst for the conversion of black money to white money for saving their TAX. They donate money in their right hand and take money from under the table in their left hand. There are many things that you can't understand. I am lying here searching for an opportunity. I know God is not so cruel. He will solve all the problems in time. Why am I talking about all these things? Many desires, daydreams, beliefs, expectations, endurance, and anticipation are still rolling on with future success. You have experienced how senior citizens, widows, divorced, and downtrodden live their lives. If you close the door to your justice, everything will die. The organization lives as they live. The choice is yours. I have some expectations from you. Don't blunder so that everyone will suffer.

I sat down under a tree. Patralekha was with me. I looked at her. Before saying something, she objected to me and said," What do you think? I have a good impression of them. But..! How people are so nasty. We belonged to an ugly slum area. Here, the place is so unsafe. Our red light is better than your gentle society. We are earning money by selling our flesh. But we are living with some self-respect. Here, people are so dangerous if required; they may shell their mother.

I will take action against them. But you tell me how I was pregnant.

Shilpa said every night, they drugged food to me. During my unconscious sleep, I was chased by a hostel warden, manager, accountant, and many more. With my unconscious mind, I was raped many times. It's my good luck I was not kidnapped. Finally, I restored my anger and burning revolution at the request of Silpa and others. I know him very well. Suppose I took action against them. Nothing will happen to them. Everyone is trapped and sold by their development strategy and rocket growth. They can be gowned to any extent for their false vanity and reputation of NGO. I did not go to any court of law due to the request of some innocent heart and distressed personality. If anything happened, the government might have a blocklist that NGO, which I didn't, because this NGO is a shelter home for many depressed, distressed, rejected, and dejected hearts. If this organization closes permanently ...where will they go? Who will take care of little orphan children? What can I do if the government is not bothered about many crimes and injustices? Better silence is the best solution to control my emotions. On that evening, I left that NGO with a bitter experience and had some emotional thoughts that I will never forget. While coming to Patralekha's house, I saw the exact truth about the Redlight area. A tremendous gathering with a melophonic atmosphere created a chaotic situation for me. The first time, I knew how every individual was hungry for sex. The public was not mature enough. They cried, bargained, shouted, roared, and emotionally appealed to many girls for intercourse because they spent money carelessly. There is no age bar among them. The father takes the daughter, the son takes the mother, and the brother takes the sister. It's an open market where sellers and buyers are not permanent. Walking on the way, I reached Patralkha's house. I rested after eating some food. Patralekha left me. I was lying in bed alone, thinking about Patralekha. Why is she helping me? Is there any evil intention?

What evil intention...everything is unveiled in my life. Still, I was remembering my past, present, and unseen future. Sometimes I think about starting my life again. To err is human. Could I change my future again? The future can be rebuilt for me. Still, I remember my panicked past. My tears rolled out to my cheek. I never oppose rolling out. This is not just a few drops of tears. It's my pain, stress, humiliation rather than suffocation from the bottom of my burning heart.

Part 8

Yes, that was the day. I agreed to my second marriage. My first husband died in a severe road accident. Looking at the rest of my life and not being a burden to my parents, I bowed to the decision of others. After all, another colorful arrangement was waiting for my life. It was not at my home. That was near to my village temple. Their family members were present. I was not excited about my first marriage. If I tell you about my first marriage, it is a long story I can't digest. I never believed how men are so cruel. I got married to my first husband. He was not my faithful husband. He committed many things to my family members. He was working in the Surat textile mill. Getting some amount makes it easy to manage his monthly routine. Whether she loved me or not. I found him in the secret chambers of my house. At midnight, she left my bed and went to the room of her elder brother's wife. I did not know ..what was happening there. One day, I found them in a ashamed situation. I shouted and cried. Later, they blamed me for creating a disturbance in their family. Many complaints were raised against me. I am not self-sufficient enough to deliver a baby. The corrupt doctor and his false medical certificate proved to me that I would never be a mother in the future.

But how can I prove that my husband is not maintaining a proper conjugal life with me? During intercourse, he always used to misuse sperm. When I am opposed to doing evil things, he dominates my argument. Later on, they forced my family to Daury. I sent my husband till their demand was not fulfilled.

Alash..! It did not come to an accurate picture that I would restore myself as the groom of my 1st husband. He died in a road accident. I never know myself. Because he never treated me as his wife. I respect many theories and theses of Indian culture and tradition. But I was not bound to respect others and expect what they wanted. Why did I suffer my whole life to accept him as my beloved? I never obeyed their rituals. I treat the past as always the past. We should walk with the present and dream of the future. Later, my family members' expectations and innocent requests compelled me to go for the second mistake. My second husband was more handsome than the 1st one.

This was an auspicious moment for me for my second innings of life. I went to that podium with my family members. Their family members waited for us. Bramhin chanted mantras, and we oathed as a new couple in the presence of lord Shiva and Parvati. On that day, he took me to his house.

When I reached his house, I was shocked and

panicked. One little girl came to me and hugged me tightly and cried remarkably.

: Mum...where have you been? I have been waiting for you for a long time. I will never leave you again.

I was astonished by her soft demand and sweet appeal. Suddenly, one of their family members told them –don't cry, baby... Your mother has come back. She will always stay with you.

My mind runs with ambiguous thoughts and feelings. After some time, I asked my second husband what the baby told me.

He told me: She is my daughter. A few months before, she lost her mother, my first wife. Every night, she dreamed of her mother. From today, she will not cry like the other day. Kindly take care of my baby.

***

That was my reception night. I was astonished to see such colorful arrangements by their family members. Everyone wishes me love and care. My bedroom looked like a flower garden. Different flowers with fragrances danced around my inner heart. Somehow, I am happy with my current husband. My daughter didn't leave me one movement. Even many relatives tried to detach her from me. But she never left me. She opposed it and said – She got her mother. If she leaves me, she will lose again.

With care, I closed her to my breast and kissed her with a smile. I had never felt such trust, love, and affection toward me. Without delivering a baby, I became a mother. It wasn't easy to adjust for the first two days. I never felt like I was a second wife having one child. The crowd became thin with the increase of deep night. But the baby was lying on my lap. I asked her what her name was.

Luckyshe said.

Again, I asked – such a sweet name. Who has given your name...? It's so lovely.

She was again so silent when looking at her grandmother. Her grandmother means my mother–in–law, who humiliates her every moment. From that day, she was beneath my protection. Oh...! Sorry. I forgot to tell you what I wanted to say. Again, I asked her who had given her such a nice name. She located me in the deep, dark sky, blooming with little stars.

LuckySee my mother. Who left me? She looks at me with her twinkling eyes every night. But not coming to me. Can you tell me what my mistake was? When I went to school, she left me. She will not come again.

She cried and cried. I have no ward and did not try to be convinced by reality. I said Listen...your mum was not angry with you. She is sitting on the top of the sky...so that she can see you every moment, whether in school or the house. She is watching you all the time.

Somehow, she was convinced. To divert the sad movement, I recited rhymes. After some time, she slept. I took her to my bedroom. She slept near to me. Surendra has already been waiting for me for a long time.

Surendra: why did you get here? You know our auspicious day!

Me: I smiled ...and told you don't be afraid. Lucky will not wake up. She is in a deep sleep. I committed to her not leaving like her mother.

Surendra: yes...I liked this...my baby.

Surenrda hugged me and gave me a tight, sweet kiss. We both blazed with burning fire. We both enjoyed the whole night. Nowadays, I am not so romantic or interested in escalating such secrets. But I have no feelings like I did in previous days. I manage my family very well. Sometimes, the Cold War ran behind due to my daughter, who was with me, and my mother-in-law. My daughter was fully protected under my safe protection. Surendra also scolded me for my blind support. I did not care about that. I was not only falling in love with my second husband but also with my daughter. So, one day, Surendra slapped me in front of her mother. Looking at our argument and fight, his mother was happy.

By the way, my life was running better than before. Once in the morning, I suffered from severe vomiting. My mother was astonished. I was taken to hospital. The doctor advised some clinical tests and reports. The doctor confirmed positive signs. I was pregnant. My body and mind are becoming relaxed and joyful with celestial happiness. But I did not understand by looking at the sorry figure of my husband, Surendra. After some time, we both returned home with medicine. While on the way home, I was getting hungry. We both went to a roadside motel. At that time, I asked Surendra what had happened to you. Are you looking upset? This was the happiest moment for both of us. Why so sorry, figure. You are going to be a father.

I have already become a father. I did not want to be there again, Surendra said. I became upset. What happened to him? I have never heard such a word. I was forced to escalate the truth from him. The truth was that I was her bed partner but not my life partner. My position in their family is like a caretaker, even not as a second wife or stepmother. She didn't want me as her spouse. She cared for me as I cared for her baby and family members.

I digest everything, but one thing I will never forget is that she didn't want any child from me. I am the third person in their family. He married me not as his wife. Wife of another person. So all emotion and sentiment had just time passed. They will not accept my baby as their next generation. One day, she told me I was his second wife, not their caste and creeds. I can't be a part of their holy occasion.

So many arguments, collisions, and revolutions started

on my side to prove my dignity, chastity, integrity, and responsibility toward my family. Everything was blasted like a drop of water bubble. I convinced him we should not go against nature's decision. He forced me to go for an abortion. I strongly oppose it. But I failed to protect my unborn baby. Without my knowledge, their family members have given me a poor diet for my health. He kicked my abdomen. I was given many antipregnancy pills to flush out my blood muscles. Without knowing anything, Lucky was a silent supporter of my running tears to wipe them out. I was the only fighter to protect myself and my baby Lucky. He also maintains a distant relationship with me. No physical relationship builds between us. I confirmed from his relatives that I would never be a mother. That knowledge was garnered from my first marriage experience. How did I convince them my first husband was not correctly sex with me? He also was wasting ejaculated sperm outside rather than in my uterus. I was not feeling well. Surendra told me to go to his friend's marriage ceremony one evening. Though I have no interest, I am still bound to go with him.

After attending the marriage ceremony, I returned home with Surendra. It was not possible. On that night, Surendra was fully dunked. Other friends of Surendra helped me drop me off at home. But the situation was different. All of their friends misbehave with me. Touched my private part. I opposed them. Though Surendra was there, he was out of control.

He was fully dunked. He smiled and was not opposed. I did not know if it was my good luck or bad luck. Luckily, I escaped them, and my journey started there in Sonagachi, a small slum cottage. You tell me what I can do. My luck always locked my future.

Part 9

Suddenly, Patralekha woke up. She saw me. My eyes were tearing out. She askedn't you feeling well? Remembering your family and relatives.

Nothing...why will I be? No one is thinking about me. Why should I be? I had forgotten my past, living with a present and uncertain future.

I am also on the same path," Patralekha said.

Why did you save me and keep me aside from notorious people? I asked her.

She smiled sweetly and slowly kept my head in her palm. And say –don't be in a hurry. You will know ...wait for time. Time will solve all the problems.

If you don't mind, I will ask you something.

Yes, you must!

I went through your dairy. Why didn't you meet your family members once again? Always sending money.

I have no courage to meet them. You know how my life

is going here. We are in a slum society. No one will accept our presence there. I said …time will solve our entire problem. Wait…and wait.

OK, one day, we plan to go to your native country. Meet your family, friends, and relatives.

Ok, baba…I will. Let's go for snacks. I am feeling hungry. Come with me to a nearby restaurant.

We both went out of home and walked on the road. We heard many comments and satire. Slowly, it digests me. I didn't react like the 1st day. Everything was going smoothly. Here is a different life. I adjust to the day running.

However, I managed and adjusted there very comfortably. But I remember the terrible day with Patralekha. It was in July, and severe rain with much water blocked. The West Bengal government declared it a cyclone day for two days—a very drastic situation. No public found any corner of the road. Still, prostitutes were roaming with umbrellas here and there to attract customers. Many bargains happened to both body sellers and sex mongers under individual umbrellas. The conversion rate of success was very low. I have seen Patralekha spend her body for fifty rupees per day. Everyone was running for bread and butter on that day. The seller is more than the buyer. So, demand on that day was very low. I am not here to convince you about the demand and supply market, which is not listed in any economic survey. I felt guilty as she fed me the last six months of her income.

One day, I told Patralekha –I want to meet your family members. I want to go to your village once again.

No one will accept either of us. –she said in a rude voice.

Why not Didi (Sister)...you give your family money monthly. You don't know whether your finances have improved the family's financial condition. We will both go to your village to see how they are living.

I am confirmed that no one will accept us. Though you are forced...let's try it once!

After I had made various requests and approaches, Patralekha agreed with me. One day, we decided to go to her village in the district of Murshidabad. From Shealdah station, we started our train journey the whole night. In the morning, we reached Rajapur, a small town in the Murshidabad area. When we reached their village, people looked like we were coming from another planet. I know some people were knowingly avoiding Patralekha and just throwing an unwanted smile. She has also given the same response. At last, we reached home. Her family members asked many questions. No one asked about what happened to her. I tried to convince her family members.

Nothing changed. All are stuck with their traditional mindset. Her brother and mother were blamed as before. Everyone warned her to leave their village. Patralekha became helpless. None of them want to know what happened to her. Why did she become a prostitute by chance or by choice? What a strange society this is! The family receives her monthly money but does not receive it as a member, as she is an unwanted guest for them. Love, emotion, and sentiment have no value. She turns back from home. On the way, we went to her dance teacher's house in Patralekha—a small BHK cottage building. A lady was sitting on the veranda. We both reached there.

The lady cordially invited us, and we went into her room. A person was lying in bed. Patralekha identifies as her teacher. I asked –what happened to your husband?

That lady was silent. Didn't speak again. Unwanted tears came out from both the corners of her eyes.

What happened ...? Why are you crying, mam. Patralekha asked.

My husband is suffering from a severe disease. None of our relatives come home. We are devastated by society.

Unknowingly, I asked –what happened to Sir? Why is she suffering? What happened to him? Why is no one coming to your house? Is there any relation to this disease?

He is affected by AIDS.

The first time I heard about this disease.

Please forget all past matters. I apologize for my mistake.

Patralekha: It's not my mistake, sir. It's a blunder. Only for you did my life path turn into a slum life. One day, you left me. I was suffering alone. Time will not leave you. As of now, you are alone. No one is with you. Every action has an equal and opposite reaction.

Teacher – yes, I am punished by God. I apologize for it.

Patralekha Imagine sir. How many false commitments played with little sentiments? You killed the trust of many innocents. You not only played my chastity but also with the trust of many girls. You are the curse epitome of guru culture (Teaching profession). Still, I am abandoned by my family, relatives, and society. I tried to come back ...but it didn't happen. I am a brand among prostitutes. You are a brand of unwanted disease. I am the first branded prostitute, and you are also the first branded AIDS patient in my village or locality. Hate, detestation, and humiliation are the property of both. We have earned it in our lives.

Suddenly, the wife of the dance teacher fell at the feet of Patralekha. Cried about husband's mistake. And apologized to her. The mind of Patralekha changed. She became cool by looking at the running tears of that lady.

Teacher's wife-Your sin may spoil my family. We are already suffering. At least save us. Your teacher is the backbone of our family. But not the whole family. Love us from the soft corner of your hearts. My husband will no longer be there after some days. I know all the past matters.

Patralekha cried and cried. After some time, she cools down. We interact with their children and other members, including the teacher's son, who is studying at Maulana Azad College Kolkata. Due to financial problems, he could not attend the final year exam. Patralekha realized all these things. Finally, she has made a bold decision. She gave a bank cheque of seventy-five thousand to the teacher's son. Last, he gave some hard cash to the teacher for his treatment. Though they felt ashamed, they received it as a token of help. We had lunch there, and we met a dance teacher.

PatralekhaSir..., I respect you as my God. But you do not deserve to get this respect. Due to my family condition and financial crisis, I went to a slum society. Though I try to return, my situation and surroundings do not compel me. I helped my family indirectly, but they didn't expect my respect. This is my last visit. I will not pray to God for your happy recovery. As you show ...so you reap. You have to suffer like this as many hearts cry. I may not come to my village. Thank you.

After that, Patralekha left that house without looking back. I followed her. While on the way near the riverside bank, I asked Patralekha.

Why are we walking on this riverside?

Just come with me. Remember, I told you I would

have cleared all your doubts one day. This is the river bank where I spent my childhood days. This river is famous for interborder transportation. There is tight security. There is still illegal work going on.

How is it possible? How do you know?

In our village, many people are farmers. Goat farming and cattle farming are just showing to society. Some agents send cows to Bangladesh along this river. They take cows for cow feed near the riverside. Bangladeshi people take those cows and sell them to the market. For each cow, they get ten thousand. India is a beefselling market for Bangladeshis.

I was astonished to hear this. Openly cow exporting is happening nowadays. With this discussion, we reached the house. The door was closed. We knocked again and again. One lady was coming from the field. Looking at us, she was looking happy. She came very forcefully and hugged Patralekha. They both tightly hugged each other. After some time, they both cried. I assured both of them.

Sneha-How are you Patralekha? After long decades, you came to meet me. Still, you remember my friendship.

Patralekha-How I will forget Sneha. You are my other heart.

Sneha: Yes, we are the two faces of one coin. Once upon a time, we qualified for a state-level competition. My bad luck was that I was unable to participate.

Patralekha- This was not your bad luck. Good luck. You imagine and compare your life and mine.

Sneha -Yes, I know that bastard dance master spoiled your life. One day, I slapped him on the open stage. He never tried to misbehave with me. You know how God has given the proper treatment. But don't forget your commitment.

"If you had a heroine, I would have got a chance to work in the film industry. My dream is not fulfilled."

PatralekhaDon't discuss the past. It hurts. Don't be panic. Life is such a diary. Once it is written, it never changes.

Suddenly, Sneha turned back to me and looked at a glance. I was astonished. What a strange. Eighty percent of my face mixed with Sneha's face. We are both the same or twins created by God. I have seen myself on her face. Patralekha introduced both of us. A lovely moment, I realized. After some time, the husband of Sneha's daughter came. We had a pleasant time with their family. Sneha's husband gave us worm treatment. We had dinner, and her husband came to drop us at the railway station. We came back by train and returned to Kolkata. Still, I was in doubt when Patralekha told me to clear all my doubts. Still, I was in a dilemma.

The next day, Patralekha suffered severe vomiting. I advise her to meet a doctor. She may have any food indigestion. But she refused to meet a doctor.

This is not the first day of vomiting. It has been continuing for the last fifteen days. Leave it. Today we will both go to the bank. I will open your account. I will give some money to you for your future.

why....? It's not required for me! I am happy with you. I have no past...I am running with an uncertain future.

Everything is OK. But the reality is something different.

After lunch, we went to the Bank near the Sovabazar metro. We went there. There was no such crowd on that premises. Patralekha went into the manager's chamber. I also followed her. There was no such indifference among staff and the public. Everyone comes with their purpose for banking work, and all staff cooperates. Patralekha introduced me to the manager. He gave me a savings bank account opening form. Patralekha added me as a nominee to her account. We both went to the locker room. She opened her locker and showed her many gold items, including where, when, and how she got them. Each of the ornaments has secret and interesting stories. I felt she was a branded icon once upon a time. But now she was spending her body at a cost of little money. I also opened a new SB account. I remember that day she told me that money is nothing in the world, but without money, you can't do anything. So, money is sweeter than honey. That day, I felt money is vital in our daily life.

She has money........! So, she was respected and cared for by the bank. I visit the bank daily and interact with the branch manager and their staff. I became a family member there. In the evening hours, sometimes I take Snax for them. One of the staff was very close to me. His name is Rounak. I don't know why he liked me, but I do. Gradually, I fell in love with him. I went to the bank and met him. Many a time, I operated a locker on behalf of Patralekha. Raunak assisted me in opening her locker with the primary key. The maximum time she kissed me in that locker room. We hugged each other. But everything is behind the camera.

Rounak joined as a probationary officer. One day, she called me to Victoria Park. We enjoyed the whole day under the tree's shadow. I have seen many a couple of friends coming to spend time there. We went to Dakhineswari Devi temple, Birla Planetarium, Millennium Park, and more during the holiday. I enjoyed my love life with him as much as I did with you. I have seen another Pritam in his eyes. My life path will change with Raunak's entry into my life. But that has not happened. One day, I returned home in the late evening. I did not find Patralekha. Suddenly I was scared and searched here and there... Where has she been? Neighbors' told me that she was admitted to the hospital. I went there—the situation I can't express. I went to Patralekha and sat near to her. She looked at me and asked.

Come...., Latika. How is Rounak? She took you

permanently. Then, I will die comfortably.

why..... Are you thinking about me? Am I not yours? Why do you care about me? Is there any difference between us?

Don't be upset...I didn't want to disturb your golden time. I think you will have a pleasant future, which I do not have!

This life and future are already dedicated to you. Why didn't you inform us when it happened? Yes..., I am not yours. So you ...didn't!

Why are you getting upset, Latika? I have been suffering for the last eight months.

Still, I am not clear about what happened to my sister. What is that disease?

I am suffering from severe cancer. I no longer have a life like you.

Suddenly, tears ran out from my eyes. Sky falling on my head....earth running out from my feet. Why is my life going like this? Where I have faith and trust.....my luck burst. How unfortunate I am!

Why am I telling this ...you know? One day, I went to Rounak's house for a proposal for my marriage. But their family member humiliates and betrays me as I am from a red light area. Rounak did not respond like before. I returned home and sat with an upset mind juxtaposed to

Patralekha. She was suffering from severe chronic pain. Somehow, I was relieved with an injected painkiller. I was suffering from mental stress and Patralekha with physical pain. Looking at my mental condition, Patralekha

motivates my moral sense and ethos.

Patralekha assured me not to cry...keep patience. I hugged Patralekha again and again. She also kissed me very carefully. Yes ...I did not notice many times she suffered from mild fever and vomiting. She neglected that as a routine disease. I donate my blood on that day as her hemoglobin rate decreases to 3.6. After two days, we returned from the hospital. Patralekha lay down in bed. I sat near to her. Her health deteriorated day by day. Many times, she required blood. I did not arrange donors for free of cost. Who would give blood to a prostitute? Everyone expects something in exchange for something. One day, I went to the bank to withdraw some money. I did not find Rounak there. I asked the branch manager. He told Rounak to get transferred to another state. I did not see him in my next life. After getting the cash, I then went home. Patralekh was sleeping. I gave her some medicine. She woke up and sat on the back support of a pillow.

Patralekha: I know society is like this! When I was a revenue-generating item, everyone ran to me. How much ...it's too much. My body sells like the trading market. Now ...no single penny...even any sympathy. You know... Latika! Why are people close to us? They get free sex instead of a girlfriend or paid friend.

You are right, sister. I did not go with Rounak for my burning sexual desire, and I needed a life partner. Why am I? Why has my luck turned into bad luck? I am not fortunate by birth like you. Still, I am in a dilemma. Why do you trust me as an unfortunate girl? Please tell me ...why..... So much sympathy for me.

She smiled and did not say anything.

Patralekha: Wait and wait...time will solve everything. One thing I expect from you. Will you keep my last wish?

Me: What?

Patralekha: don't spend my savings. It's a waste of money. Many things happen on your backside. I have no long life. You will keep my savings and live happily for the rest of your life. Don't worry about my treatment. I want to see your smiling face for the rest of my life. I did not do anything for others—at least something for you.

Me: I can't understand...what you are telling me and your purpose!

I first refused by listening to this oath, but I was bound to respect her commitment. She strictly told me not to use her savings, but how could I get her treatment? For her treatment again, a packet of blood is required. I searched for a donor exchange by telling her name. No one shows sympathy for her. Everyone demands an exchange for the desire for sex. I have no option. Without informing Patralekha, I collected a blood donor by sacrificing my body. The first time, I did illegal work for a noble cause. I don't know if that was right or wrong. This was my first step toward the prostitution world. By the way, I became a body donor, sex worker, or prostitute in everyone's eyes. But I did not care about others' feelings or respect. I have negative feelings towards the male species. One morning, I got a phone call from the hospital that Patralekha had died. I shocked. Suddenly, I ran to the hospital. No one was with me. I took her body to a graveyard—a dead body burned on fire. After a few minutes, everything turned into ash. Finally, no one was there except me. I collected ass in a pot and went home.

Part 10

I did not sleep the whole night. Her blessing hand was removed from my head. I was living as an orphan lady. After a few days, a call came from the bank. I went and met the branch head. The manager called me to his cabin and gave me all the documents for Patralekha. Mager helped me and transferred the documents to my name. Before Patralekha died, she nominated my name. I am unfortunate to save her life. I got a good manager. He is not only a bank manager but also an author. You know him .... Sometimes his stories and articles are published in magazines. He is a famous author like Chetan, Biraj, Rabin, Sinui, and Sidharth Nagarkar, and he is a struggling writer. He is Tapan, a banker, and an author. I told my whole life story about how my life came from a village to a market. Why did I become a prostitute not by choice but by chance? My life story touched his inner heart very much. He told me to write my biography into a novel. If this novel is published, you should have purchased it for the memories of our love.

I am spending my life like a prisoner. No one is with me. Through my window, I saw the busy life of the Kolkata metro. Sometimes, my door is knocked on by many clients. Other prostitutes also used my room on a rent basis. They earned money, but I did not charge anything. Sometimes, they paid monthly rent to the house owner. My upset mind was not restored to normal. Suddenly, my mind was struck by Patralekha's diary. I opened the rest of his diary, the part which I had not read. I was astonished by going through that.

"Yes..., I am Patralekha, a famous prostitute who works for money or to satisfy others' sexual desires. I don't know if the dedication of my life destroys others' family lives or protects many rape cases in India. To save a woman from all the rapists, I met Latika at midnight. I took her to my home for her choice. I lost my younger daughter, who the rapist killed. Notorious victims murdered her. Still, she cried in my dream....please help...me...help ....me. From that day, every night, I went to different places with many prostitutes. Not only do I earn money, but I also kill many sex mongers who are the garbage of our country. After killing them, I ran through them onto the national highway road. The next day, police complained about a road accident—many thanks to the Andhra truck driver who helped me clean the notorious garbage from India. I don't know whose family was affected, destroyed, and spoiled. For the sake of my country, I did a job well, which is not my duty but my responsibility as an Indian. The death of my little sister's face looked like Latika's. So I cared and helped a lot till the end of my life. God gave punishment in the form of cancer. Every action has an equal and opposite reaction. The severe pain I had given to many sex-hunger clients reflected on me in the form of the disease. But I saved the lives of many women by using sex workers. I did not want to meet my family, friends, and relatives. They did not accept me. So I left them a long year ago. My sweet sister Latika forced me to go home again. I have no interest. But I met them, which was my last visit. In my life, I excused the husband of Sneha, who had raped me many times in my friend's absence. Because of my excuse, my little sister was staying in Sneha's house, and she was the mystery of my father's mistake. I didn't want to open my father's secret. So Sneha also likes my sister and friend."

After going through this diary, I stagnate like a dead stone. I got the hidden truth behind Patralekha. Every day, I dreamed about Patralekha. I was suffocated by staying in this area. Every day, an atmosphere gets vituperate and vicious with a cruciate mind. I can't live without family, but my family does not accept me. Why do I save money for the rest of my life? I did not expect a long life, but my life should be great. Everyone in the world cheated on me and grabbed me with time and tides. In a male-dominated society, I am never trusted by human beings. Why is my slum body dedicated to others better than going for a light of devotion? I have decided to die. Death is my ultimate solution. Because ...., life after death is better than suffocated life.

Thanks............ Pritam...... have patience to listen to my dread feelings and afflictive thoughts.

You may accept or reject.

It's your choice.

It's the last letter of Latika.....

Goodbye...forever!!!!!!!

Your Latika.

Part 11

From The Voice Of The Author:

"One day, Latika came to my office. I offered to sit in a customer's chair. She hands over the locker key with another certificate of deposit and a savings passbook. Give one letter with the requested information—my various requests and appeals she rejected. In the letter, she asked me to use her money wisely. She is going to die on that day. After she left, I went to locker no.11, where I got this letter. I took all the gold and other ornaments. I carried some cash and gold to her stepdaughter Lucky and others to Sneha. She told me to use her money wisely, which a banker knows better. She refused to give money to any charitable organization, left the bank, and told me she would leave this world and not try to find her later. She took Lord KRISHNA's gold statue, which was kept in her locker. I was in doubt as to why she left other gold except that God. Her journey started on a spiritualistic path. While coming from the office that evening, I saw her at the Dharmatala (Kolkata) bus terminal. Latika was waiting for a bus with her bag and the ash of patralekha on the other hand. I didn't remember that bus number, but

*it was going to Mayapure, a famous ISCON temple. After that, many local customers came to the branch and discussed Latikha and whether she had died or was alive. Many discussions happened for six months. One day, I found Latika on a YouTube channel of the Kumbhamela video. She was walking in between Naga saints in a grey dress. I did not escalate more about these videos. Now, that situation is not like before—that letter I want to send her beloved Pritam. Still, I do not have his proper address. As she is staying in Banglore and working for a software company, he also married Reena. I published this book and got this **"letter of Latika from locker no11"**. A sincere appeal to my beloved readers is whether Pritam has proper contact details and which letter I have to send. "*

— ❖ —

The End

{Not end.......It's just the beginning of another imperfect love story going to happen.}

Copyright Disclaimer

Copyright Disclaimer Under section 107 of the Copyright Act 1976, allowance is made for "fair use" for purposes such as criticism, comment, news reporting, teaching, scholarship, education, and research. Fair use is permitted by copyright statutes that might otherwise be infringing. © Copyright, 2021, TAPAN MAJHI, All rights reserved.

No part of this book may be reproduced, stored in a retrieval system, or transmitted in any form by any means, optical, chemical, manual, photocopying, recording, electronic, mechanical, magnetic, or otherwise, without the prior written consent of its writer. The opinions/ contents expressed in this book are the sole of the author and do not represent the publisher's opinions/ standings/ thoughts. Printed in India Copyright © 2021 TAPAN MAJHI. All rights reserved, all rights reserved.

No part of this publication may be reproduced, stored in a retrieval system, or transmitted in any form or by any means, electronic, mechanical, recording, or otherwise, without the author's prior written permission. This book has been published with all reasonable efforts to make the material error-free after the author's consent. The author of this book is solely responsible and liable for its Content, including but not limited to the views, representations, descriptions, statements, information, opinions, and references ["Content"].

The publisher does not endorse or approve the Content of this book or guarantee the reliability, accuracy, or completeness of the Content published herein. The publisher and the author make no representations or warranties concerning this book or its contents. The author and the publisher disclaim all such representations and warranties, including, for example, warranties of merchantability and educational or medical advice for a particular purpose. In addition, the author and the publisher do not represent or warrant that the information accessible via this book is accurate, complete, or current.

XX   XX

Know more about TAPAN MAJHI by

Website: tapanmajhi.com
https://facebook.com/tapanmajhi.kumar
amazon.com/author/tapanmajhi
Mail: tapansahitya@gmail.com
Threads/Instagram: tapanmajhivlog

https://www.amazon.com/dp/B09WND8PDZ

https://www.amazon.in/dp/B09TG5QVPX/ref=cm_s w_r_apan_NEF8R7Y0V14WGT2ASZBG (India link)

https://www.amazon.com/dp/B09PB9LKVT

https://www.amazon.in/dp/B09PB9LKVT/ref=cm_s w_r_apan_NH8FJF4EV73JRJ99FS9Z _(India link)

https://amzn.in/d/aQmUogz   (Paperback)

https://www.amazon.in/gp/product/B0BGJJR9G6?notRedire ctToSDP=1&ref_=dbs_mng_calw_1&storeType=ebooks

https://amzn.in/d/ivEpCcD   (eBook)

http://www.amazon.in/gp/offerlisting/B09BW74TQP /?seller=A3H5P1VWN5G119&ref=myi_listid_offer
(India link)

http://tapanmajhi.com/

Thank you